ALL THAT REMAINS

THE DI BENJAMIN KIDD THRILLERS
BOOK 12

GS RHODES

DARK SHIP CRIME

ALL THAT REMAINS

ALSO BY GS RHODES

READING ORDER

A reader reached out to be recently asking about the order in which the DI Benjamin Kidd and DS Zoe Sanchez books are to be read in as the two series run concurrently. There are links between the two series, and moments where the plots crossover (normally in phone calls between the two detectives.) It isn't essential for them to be read in this order, or even for both series to be read, but below is that reading order for anyone interested in getting that fully rounded reading experience.

———

When You're Smiling (DI Benjamin Kidd #1)
Just Keep Breathing (DI Benjamin Kidd #2)
Your Best Shot (DI Benjamin Kidd #3)
Be My Baby (DI Benjamin Kidd #4)

CONTENTS

CHAPTER
ONE

Nina Hawkins had done something she knew she wasn't supposed to do. It was against every fibre of her being, and the guilt she was carrying with her would likely haunt her for the rest of her life. But if she kept drinking, then maybe she wouldn't have to feel it. That would be something.

There had been things in her life that weren't quite right, things that had needed drastic action in order for them to improve, so she had done what she thought was best. It might not have felt right in the moment, maybe it still didn't, but maybe it would eventually—maybe, as time passed, things would feel better.

"It was my only option," she said to herself as she got ready for a night out with her housemates.

She wiped the mirror and looked at her complexion. She looked tired. The sleepless nights were starting to catch up to her. It was going to take a mountain of concealer to cover those eye bags. But it was worth it because, despite the guilt, there was a strange feeling of freedom that filled her up. She had gotten away. And there would be people out there who would thank her for it. Whether consciously or not, they would.

It will catch up to you eventually, she thought. That was the prevailing thought, that was what was keeping her up at night, that it would all catch up to her in the end. But so what if it did? She would accept the consequences. For now, she would just enjoy herself.

"Come on, Nina, quit hogging the bathroom!" Her flatmate Paige was knocking on the door, no doubt wrapped in a towel, waiting to hop in the shower after hearing Nina shut the water off.

Nina opened the door and fixed Paige with an exhausted kind of grin. As expected, Paige was in her towel. "It takes a lot of time for me to get ready, Paige, you know this about me."

"I do," Paige replied. "But I also know that we only get so much hot water, and if I have to take a cold shower, I'm going to shove you down those stairs."

Nina shook her head. "So mean," she said. "Your turn anyway, no need for murder."

"We're going to The Snake Pit, babes, I wouldn't speak quite so soon. You know what the men there are like."

Nina giggled nervously. "Don't say that," she said. "Like I'm not stressed enough without thinking about the creeps at The Snake Pit."

"Sorry, forgot you're not sleeping so well," Paige said. "Want to talk about it?"

"Christ, no," Nina replied. "Just boring work stuff. You know how life is."

Paige nodded. She did know. She knew all about Nina's problems. Well... not all, but she knew about a lot of them. There were several that they shared, and would lament over their Sainsbury's Basics evening meals because they couldn't afford anything else. The fact that they were going out tonight was only because yesterday was payday.

Yes, they probably should have been saving all that, but... they deserved a bit of time off, an evening out. They deserved it.

"About the other night—"

"No," Nina interrupted quickly. "Not now, please, Paige, not now."

"Okay," Paige said. "You just worry me, Nina, that's all. I don't want you to be dealing with all that yourself."

"I'm doing fine. Besides, we shouldn't be thinking about that, we're meant to be out enjoying ourselves," Nina said. "Come on, get yourself showered or we'll never get out of here."

Paige laughed. "That might be for the best." Paige paused in the doorway. "Are you sure?"

Nina swallowed, steeled herself, and stood up straight to her full height. "It's fine," she said. "So damn fine. Now get ready, or you know Sienna will come and shove you out of the way to get into the bathroom first."

Paige shuffled into the bathroom and shut the door behind her. The shower turned back on, no doubt roasting hot as Paige steamed herself into oblivion.

Nina let out a breath and went to her bedroom. She loved Paige more than anything in the world. She knew all of her darkest secrets and had got her through some of her darkest moments. She didn't know what she'd do without her, and hoped she would never have to find out.

Paige started singing in the shower, and Nina couldn't help but laugh. It wasn't worth dwelling on the darkness. The darkness could wait. For now, they were going to have a nice evening out. They deserved that, didn't they? Yes. , they did. They would enjoy tonight, because who knew if they were even promised a tomorrow.

WHEN DID THINGS BECOME BLURRY? IT WAS HARD TO tell. There was a part of Nina that could almost remember which drink had tipped her over the edge, which one had brought her to this strange sense of freedom and oblivion. But what was the use of remembering when she could barely tell where she was?

The Snake Pit.

That's where she was.

The song that was playing was... What was it? Some techno remix of a pop song that had come out before she was born. She could feel the bass humming through her feet, vibrating in her chest, and she danced and danced and danced. It was wonderful. It was freedom. It was not thinking about...

Except, now she was thinking about it.

She needed to push that away, so she took another sip and another and another until the glass was empty. And then the glass was gone, the plastic container somewhere on the floor in a sea of people dancing, writhing, partying.

Where were her friends? Where had they gone? Paige was off kissing someone. She'd seen that, so who knew where she'd ended up?

She took out her phone. She couldn't see the screen. It was blurry. She rubbed it on her top, but it was still blurry. It was her eyes that were blurry. Not the phone screen.

She pocketed it again and started outside, stumbling through the crowd until the cold night air hit her like a runaway train. It nearly floored her. Were it not for the kind stranger behind her, propping her up again, she might have done herself an injury.

"Thankyousomuch," she slurred, stepping out and away from the club and towards the riverside. She breathed in the cool air, listening to the distant pulsing of the music in the club, the distant zooming of cars in the distance, and she paused.

Nina wanted to sit down, so she did, just on the stairs, just for a minute, staring down at the river as it rushed by. This was the peace she craved. This was the kind of night she should have been trying to have instead of one out partying with friends. She wanted peace, and it was coming.

So Nina Hawkins closed her eyes.

She opened them with a start, breathing in a gasp of air, but... the air wouldn't enter her lungs. Something was stopping her from breathing. And she saw the figure overhead, the looming darkness, and she could see the arms coming from it, the hands wrapped around her throat. And she tried to scream. She tried her best, but no... nothing. The edges of her vision started to go dark as the air couldn't reach her lungs, as the world started to disappear around her.

And she thought of her friends in the club,

wondering where she was, the friends she had been through so much with, the friends she'd done unspeakable things for. And they would never know. They'd never realise. Because Nina Hawkins was dying.

CHAPTER
TWO

Detective Inspector Benjamin Kidd had finally made it back to Kingston. He'd taken the long way around, his sabbatical taking him to places that he hadn't necessarily expected to go and taking him on adventures that... well... If he was totally honest with himself, he knew he shouldn't have been going on those adventures either. But he was back in one piece and things felt... different.

When he got back to the house a month ago, his sister, Liz, had done a brilliant job of putting up the Christmas decorations in time for their arrival. The place had looked like a winter wonderland, even if it had been piss-wet and grey outside. But his home didn't feel quite like his home anymore. He'd not lived there for quite a long time, and that had shifted things in him.

It wasn't that there was something wrong with

the house, it was just as lovely and homely as it had been when they'd left. The problem was that it didn't feel like home anymore. Too much had happened. Too much had changed.

Of course, I'd find a problem three seconds after walking into the house, he'd thought. *Like I don't have enough on my plate.*

The days passed by in something of a flurry. He'd had dinner with his best friend, Detective Sergeant Zoe Sanchez, and they caught up about everything that had been going on with her, updates in the team, that kind of thing. He went and talked to Detective Chief Inspector Weaver, who set him up with Occupational Health and a fitness test, which he absolutely wasn't looking forward to.

"I knew you shouldn't have stopped running," John said when he came back from that particular meeting.

"I mean, I did get injured rather a lot."

"Yes, I remember," John replied. "Maybe that will teach you not to throw yourself in headfirst."

"We've been together long enough for you to realise that's never going to happen," Kidd replied.

He worked hard in the run-up to the fitness test, only taking a bit of time off over Christmas, and managed to scrape his way through it in the new year. The years were catching up with him, and how he was meant to get through that again when it rolled around was beyond him.

Sure, he could keep going on runs and stay in shape, but every time he tried to do that, something would come along and derail him. Either some mammoth case that meant all his time and brain power was occupied by that, or he ended up getting into some scrape that laid him out flat.

Maybe he did need to take it a little easier.

Today's run would be the last before he went back to work for real. He'd got the all-clear from Occupational Health. Weaver had called him up and told him to get back into the office, that it was all systems go on the work front. He'd be lying if he said he wasn't a little bit excited.

He made his way downstairs in his running gear to find John in the kitchen, filling a flask with what looked like tea.

"Bloody hell, going out again?" he asked with a smirk. "You passed the test, Ben. You don't need to keep running."

"Trying to stay on top of it this time."

"How long will that last?"

"Until a case file hits my desk," Kidd replied. "You alright? You left me to sleep?"

"Woke up early, so came downstairs to check on some emails that came through over Christmas."

"Who the bloody hell was emailing over Christmas?"

"My psycho boss," he replied with a smirk. "You know how she gets. A thought pops into her head, and next thing you know, it's in my bloody inbox. I think she's happy I'm coming back to the office today."

The implication there was that John wasn't as happy about going back.

He worked for Westway Press, a big London publisher that did everything from romance to crime to sci-fi and beyond. John had been editing a crime book when his client was murdered, then he was targeted as well, only narrowly being saved from the same fate, and... well... it was part of the reason they'd ended up taking off on their little road trip for a bit.

He'd managed to keep working away for a bit while they weren't in Kingston, dialling into meetings and such when he needed to, but now things were getting real. They were both going back to work. Life was about to have some semblance of a routine again.

"Take it easy, maybe," Kidd said. He hated seeing John stressed out and worried. He was such a nice man, such a kind soul. The last thing he wanted to see was someone he cared so much about, someone he loved, getting bogged down by work. "If it helps, we can start planning a holiday when I get back tonight. That's one way to take your mind off work. Start planning to be away from it."

"You on a holiday?" John said with a snort. "We

just tried to take a holiday, and you ended up working with the local force."

"Yeah, not ideal, that," Kidd replied. "Sorry."

"It's okay. I was working anyway, and you enjoy it," he replied with a laugh. "But we can't tonight, remember? We're having dinner with Liz."

"Oh God, are we?"

"When did I become your PA as well as your boyfriend?" John said. "We're going round to hers at seven, having dinner, proper New Year's catch up. Please don't leave me alone with your sister."

"You love Liz."

"I do love Liz," John replied with a laugh. "But she's still your sister, and we haven't spent that much time together, so I'll be deathly nervous if it's just me, her, and Greg."

"I'll be there," Kidd said, stepping towards John and giving him a kiss. "Good luck today. Not that you need it. Maybe don't rip your boss's head off."

"I'm not you," John replied. "Though, now if that happens, I'll be the prime suspect. Damn. Have to get rid of her another way."

Kidd said his goodbyes and made his way outside, breaking into a run. He took a different route today, down towards Fairfield Park, running around it a few times before circling back. He slowed down and then stopped to stretch before starting a cool-down walk home.

His phone rang in his pocket, interrupting his

music, and he took it out to see that it was Liz, probably to make sure he was actually coming tonight. He looked forward to smugly saying he was. PA John McAdams to the rescue.

"Hey, Lizzy," Kidd said, more than a little out of breath. He really did need to keep running after all. "What can I do for you this fine morning?"

"You can cut the chipper attitude for a start. Where are you?" she asked, incredulous.

"Out for a run," he said. "Why?"

"Oh you make me sick," she replied. "It's minus two, Ben. Why on God's green earth are you out for a run?"

"Because I barely passed my fitness test, and I'd rather not collapse while I'm on the job today if I can help it," he replied. "Was there anything I could help you with, or did you just call to berate me?"

"Alright, alright," she said, white flag raised. "I was just calling to check in, make sure you were still coming tonight."

"Of course we are," he said. "Would be rude not to."

"Especially at such short notice when I'm doing a roast and already started prepping it."

"Bloody hell, it's like a second Christmas," Kidd replied. "How are things? How are the kids? Did you have any New Year's plans?"

"My New Year's plans were: pyjamas by eight pm, fall asleep in front of the TV, wake up to watch the fireworks, and go to bed," she replied. "A very successful evening, if you must know."

They kept talking on his walk home. This was one of the reasons he was glad to be back, being closer to Liz again. They'd not talked much while he'd been away, a combination of Kidd just putting everything about Kingston out of sight and out of mind, and Liz wanting to give him some space. She didn't want to intrude on his time away, and he had appreciated that. Even if he had found work to do off his own back.

He hung up once he got back inside, sticking the kettle on while he had a quick shower and got himself ready for the day. With a cup of tea in a flask that John had bought him for Christmas, he made his way to the station, ready for his first proper day back.

He wouldn't admit it to anyone, but he was excited to be back in Kingston, part of the team once again, and while he didn't wish ill fortune on anyone, he was excited to sink his teeth into a new case. He was a new man. Things were going to be better. He had decided.

CHAPTER
THREE

The walk to the station was fairly pleasant. He was starting a little later today, so the traffic on the roads was minimal. The school children had already vanished into their first classes of the day, and that initial hustle and bustle had passed. He could be alone with his thoughts, sipping his tea as he went.

There was still an ominous air to the building. The concrete block opposite the Rose Theatre seemed imposing against the skyline. It practically blended into the heavy cloud coverage this morning.

It looked like it was either going to rain or snow, Kidd wasn't sure.

Typical, we can't get a white Christmas, but we can have a white January, he thought, digging his free hand deeper into his pocket. He needed gloves. He should have asked for them for Christmas. Why did he always think of the perfect gift after the fact?

He walked into the station reception and was greeted with the biggest smile from the station officer. She was on the phone and gave him the one-minute finger. He knew better than to defy her, so he waited, letting her finish her call.

"Well, well, well, as I live and breathe, look who is finally back," she said.

"Good morning, Diane," he said. "This is the kind of greeting I was hoping for. You can bet your life Weaver isn't about to roll out the red carpet."

"Well, he should," she said. "I'd heard you were coming back. People had said you'd been in and had meetings and such, but I'd not seen you, so I didn't think it was true."

"Sorry, Diane, I am back, unfortunately."

"What do you mean, 'unfortunately?'" she replied. "I've missed you. Missed you causing trouble around here, it's been too quiet."

Kidd laughed. "From what I've heard, it's not been quiet at all," he replied. "But it's always nice to be missed. Who was on the phone?"

Diane rolled her eyes. "Who do you think? Some members of the press are already hounding me for details of what's going on by the river." She let out a sigh. "Honestly, they think I was born yesterday. Can't help but try their luck and try and get information out of me. No chance. They'll find out when everyone else does."

Kidd needed her to rewind for a second. "What's going on by the river?" he asked. "Something I should know about? I didn't walk that way this morning, I must have missed it?"

"See, now you're trying to get me to reveal my sources," she said with a smirk. "Don't actually know that much about it at this stage, but there are Uniforms down there already, Forensics on the way, it's all go go go." She eyed him carefully. "If I didn't know better, I'd say you'd been hoping you were going to walk into something like this today."

"I don't wish for anyone to need my help," Kidd said, but then lowered his voice. "But it would be a bloody boring job if no one did, eh?"

Diane laughed, and Kidd said his goodbyes before making his way through that familiar door and into the backrooms of Kingston station. People said hello as he walked past, welcoming him back, A couple asked him where he'd been. Some of them didn't seem to know he'd been anywhere, and that was kind of the most beautiful part of it. Something major can be happening in your life, and it can feel like the centre of the whole universe, but you're a blip on someone else's radar. It puts things in perspective, makes things feel a little less high-pressure.

He made his way into the Incident Room, and

was greeted by several pairs of eyes looking up to see him come in. It really did feel good to be back.

"Good morning, Boss." Detective Sergeant Zoe Sanchez was at her desk already, curly hair pulled back into a ponytail, eyes trained on him, mischief glistening in her smile. "What time do you call this? You take some time off and suddenly get to have slacker's hours?"

"Alright, alright," he said. "Morning."

The rest of the team said good morning too; Detective Constable Janya Ravel joined in with Zoe, ribbing him about his late start, and Detective Constable Simon Powell immediately offered him a pastry, which he happily took, and then he noticed that the new detective constable, Ashley Hale, was hanging back.

Kidd had met him already, the team having been out socialising in the past couple of weeks. They wanted to welcome him back, but also didn't want him to have to dive straight into work the second he got there. It had been nice. It made the whole first-day-back thing feel less nerve-racking.

DC Ashley Hale, who insisted on being called Ash because Ashley makes him feel like he's in trouble, greeted Kidd somewhat nervously. He was tall, gangly, and definitely standoffish now that they were in the Incident Room together. It was one thing to get to know each other socially, but they'd not worked together yet. In a lot of ways, they had things to prove to one another. Kidd needed to prove he was a decent boss, Ash needed to prove he was a competent DC.

"Nothing's come in yet, has it?" Kidd asked, making his way over to his desk and hanging his jacket on the back of it. It was almost exactly as he'd left it, despite a DI covering for him while he was away. It was completely cleared of its usual debris from whatever case he happened to be working on at that time. He knew that would change soon enough.

Zoe turned to him, eyebrow raised. "Nothing yet," she said. "We're finishing up a couple of things from our last case, tying up loose ends. Why? Have you heard something?"

"Diane mentioned something happening by the river this morning," Kidd replied. "I'd be lying if I said it didn't make me sit up and pay attention."

"I didn't walk that way," Zoe said. "Otherwise, I could have given you the gossip."

"It's going to land on someone's desk," Kidd said. "It might be ours, you never know."

"God, you really are back, aren't you?" she said.

"What do you mean?"

"Barely in the door and you're looking for a case to sink your teeth into," Zoe said. "Some things never change."

Kidd took a moment to self-reflect. Maybe things did need to change. If they didn't have anything on their plates just yet, what was the harm in a slightly easier morning? He grabbed his jacket off the back of his chair, slipping it back on.

"Bored already?" Zoe said.

"No," Kidd replied, before turning to the rest of the team. "How about breakfast?" he called out. "Before Weaver comes barrelling in here, telling us to get to work on something, we could go out, get some breakfast? Anyone?"

Powell got to his feet first. "Sounds like a plan," he said. "Why not?"

They gathered themselves, grabbing jackets and coats and scarves—it really was bitterly cold outside. They'd barely made it to the door when it swung open, the imposing form of Detective Chief Inspector Patrick Weaver filling the door frame.

He eyed them each carefully, confusion flickering across his face as he took them all in.

"Are we going somewhere?" he asked.

"Breakfast, sir," Kidd replied. "Morale and all that."

Weaver smirked. "A lovely idea," he replied. "But one that I'm afraid we're going to have to postpone." Kidd's stomach dropped out of his feet. "We're needed down by the river," he continued, before locking eyes with Kidd. "Welcome back."

CHAPTER
FOUR

The rest of the team stayed behind as Kidd and Weaver made their way down to the riverside. Even though Kidd had been hoping for this, there was always that jolt of nerves when you first got assigned a new case. You never knew what was going to be waiting for you around the next corner, and the fact that even Weaver seemed a little troubled by it told Kidd this was going to be far from easy.

"What do we have so far?" Kidd asked.

"Not a whole lot," Weaver replied. "I got the call right before I came to see you. We're getting in on the ground of this one, so it's all... It'll be a little tense."

As they turned the corner onto the riverside, a cold breeze coming in off the water and battering them in the face, Kidd could see the crowds of people gathered up ahead. People were walking past in the opposite direction, shaking their heads, frustrated by something.

And then Kidd realised.

They're being turned around, he thought. *This section of the Riverside is closed. People can't walk through.*

He looked at the restaurants as he walked past. The pub on the corner had managed to open, just outside of the cordon, but the rest of them, the ones that had no other way in or out, they were all closed, people in matching uniforms gathering in little clusters as they waited to be told whether or not they'd be opening at all.

The uniformed officers at the cordon looked like they were about to freeze to death, rosy cheeks and pink noses giving away the fact that, despite their stern expressions, this was not an ideal situation for them.

Kidd said his good mornings, flashing his badge as he stepped under the police tape and made his way to the group of people in white coveralls.

"DI Kidd, you're back." Frances Dean's voice was one of surprise. Maybe people hadn't been expecting him to return. "Bit of a troublesome one to be coming back to, I'm afraid."

"What have we got?" Weaver asked.

"Under the overpass," Frances said. "Female, early twenties, found down there in the early hours of the morning by people who had been at the club. The Snake Pit, you know it?"

"I know of it," Kidd replied. "Cause of death?"

"Not one hundred percent sure," Frances replied. "We'll need to do an autopsy because the body seems entirely intact, but there are marks around the neck. Looks like it could have been strangulation."

Kidd winced. Of all the ways to go. He'd been almost choked out on cases before, that feeling of the world closing in around you, of the blackness taking over. It was a slow death.

"Can we see her?" Weaver asked.

Frances took them towards the underpass, the light from the day cast into shadow by the bridge. The tent was practically glowing beneath the archway of stone, people in white coveralls walking around it, searching the surrounding area, taking photos.

She let them inside the tent so that they could take a look at the girl. She was young—twenties was definitely the right call there—and she was deathly pale, the life squeezed out of her by a seemingly average pair of hands around her neck. The red marks seemed more pronounced in the white light, bright and angry against her skin.

He looked at her hands, perfectly manicured nails. They'd be worth scraping for DNA in case she managed to fight off her attacker. And then he saw the wristband.

"What's that?" Kidd asked, pointing at the fluorescent strip of yellow around her wrist.

Frances reached a gloved hand down and lifted it. In faded black letters was the logo for The Snake Pit, a serpent coiled around a martini glass. So they knew where she had been. They just needed to know how she got down here and who on earth had done this to her.

"Was she just left here?"

"As far as we can tell, yes," Frances replied. "Not even tucked away to one side, she was slap-bang in the middle of the pavement. Whoever did this wanted her to be found. No effort was made to hide the body at all."

Kidd looked over at Weaver, who looked spooked. If someone wanted this body to be found, then that someone was likely sending a message. But if that was the case, who was the message for? Kidd's stomach twisted.

"Looks pretty clear that the cause of death was strangulation. Those marks are... They're angry," Kidd said. "But let us know what you find out from the autopsy."

"That's what I'm leaning towards, but it's worth testing to make sure there weren't other factors," she said.

"Thanks, Frances, I appreciate that," Kidd replied, taking the opportunity to step out of the tent and back into the open. He took a few deep breaths, gulping in the fresh air as he tried to figure out what to do next.

"What do you think?" Weaver asked.

It was the vaguest question imaginable, the kind of question that made Kidd just want to respond with "lots of things" but he resisted that urge. He could get on Weaver's back about things later. Right now, he needed to focus.

"Well," Kidd started. "Like Frances said, whoever is responsible for this wanted it to be found. You don't leave a body out in the open like that if you don't want it to be seen."

"Right."

"Right," Kidd said. "So we need to find out who our killer wanted to see it. Maybe there are friends, colleagues, something like that. Maybe people who she was with last night?"

"Where do you want to start?"

Kidd took a breath, and looked along the riverside, clocking the CCTV cameras that were there, the flats above some of the restaurants, The Snake Pit club nearby. There were a lot of options for them to look into, a lot of places for them to go from here. It wasn't going to be easy by any stretch, but the sooner they could figure out who she was and how on earth she got here, the better.

"There's a lot of coverage here," Kidd said. "Restaurants, apartments, there's all sorts. And you know The Snake Pit is going to have a decent amount of security cameras as well. Or at least, I hope that it does."

"She was there last night, so they'll have a decent track of her movements."

"If we're lucky," Kidd said. "That's where I want to start. Do we know if there are workers there yet?"

"Given what's going on, I would imagine so," Weaver said. "But if not, they'd better get down here, and fast."

"Agreed," Kidd said. "No time to waste. Let's get moving."

CHAPTER
FIVE

Over the past few years, Kidd had spent more time in clubs during the day than he had at night. He couldn't tell you the last time he'd ended up in a club at night, and he was glad for that. Seeing it in the daylight would be enough to put anyone off.

The Snake Pit was just at the end of Kingston Bridge. During the day, you could almost miss it if you didn't know it was there. At night, it was all lit up, the logo bright white and glowing, but you'd likely hear it before you saw it.

The doors were already open, a couple of uniformed officers stood at the edge of where the cordon extended. People would not be getting down to the riverside today, no chance of that at all. The amount of trouble it was all causing, whoever did this, was trying to make an impact, that much was clear. The question was, why? And who on earth would want to do something like that?

There were already people trying to look inside, trying to see what was going on. There were a couple of faces that Kidd recognised almost immediately, ones that had been to various press conferences that he had given while he'd been on the force. He could even see Joe Warrington trying to peek over people's heads to get a better look. He caught Kidd's eye, his face bursting into a smile. He was hoping for an exclusive. Kidd was going to dash those hopes.

"Kidd!" he called out, not just pulling Kidd's focus, but getting the attention of every other vulture there.

Thanks for that, Joe, Kidd thought. He made his way over to the waiting crowd, immediately being pelted with questions ranging from a simple, "What's going on?" to those asking for a formal statement, detailing exactly what had happened.

"Before anyone gets too excited, I only got this case fifteen minutes ago," he said, raising his voice over the howling wind, over the clamouring journalists. "We'll release any information we manage to get at the appropriate time, but until then, all I can ask is that you don't bother the police officers who are on this cordon. They've already been here for a while, and there are no real signs of that changing anytime soon. If you want to be useful, get them a coffee or a slice of cake; otherwise, leave them be."

Kidd turned back towards The Snake Pit, ignoring the calls behind him, the further questions, the people who had heard what he'd said, but not necessarily listened to it. They would never learn.

He stepped through the security gates of The Snake Pit, past the cloakroom, and into the main part of the club. There was a bar along one wall of the room, a dance floor spreading out before it, and a DJ booth off in the far corner. Everything was painted black, and everything seemed to be covered in a thin layer of grime. There were plastic cups on the floor, a couple of plastic shot glasses tossed off to one side.

Dotted around the edges of the space were a couple of booths, a flimsy red velvet rope in front of them, chairs covered in tattered black leather. Perhaps not the kind of thing you pay attention to when you're on a night out. They're likely just excited to be able to sit down.

God, Kidd thought. *That makes me sound old.*

Around the rest of the room were a couple of tall tables that looked sticky, even from this distance. Like if you put your hand on it, you'd peel away a layer of skin as you tried to get it off. The entire place needed to be sterilised, and there was no one around who seemed to be doing it. Was there anyone even here?

"Hello?" Kidd called out. His voice bounced around him in a way he hadn't been expecting. In the evenings, this place would be absolutely teeming

31

with people. Right now, Kidd couldn't even tell if there was somebody working.

A man poked his head out from behind the bar, appearing from behind a door. He was youngish, a boyish face with a smattering of stubble, his hair a little long and a lot scruffy. He looked exhausted, and he was wearing a pair of blue plastic gloves. The kind that Kidd and the team wore when they were searching someone's flat, when they were trying not to contaminate any of the evidence. Kidd would wager he'd been working last night and had been dragged in this morning to sort out whatever mess had happened on his watch. Kidd intended to give him a bit of a bollocking about that, for sure.

"Detective Inspector Benjamin Kidd," he said, pulling out his badge and flashing it at the young man. "Are you the person I need to be speaking to, or is there anyone more senior I should be dealing with?"

The lad raised an eyebrow. Apparently, Kidd commenting on his age was enough to get his hackles up.

"Benjamin Kidd," he said, looking the detective up and down. Kidd didn't like that, it immediately put him on edge. "I wondered if it was going to be you that I'd be dealing with. I've heard a lot about you."

"My reputation precedes me?"

"You're Zoe's friend," he said. "I'm Seth."

Kidd nodded. "Ah," he said. "Zoe's boyfriend."

"Yes."

"Hardly the ideal way for the two of us to be meeting," Kidd said. "You sure you're the only one here to deal with this?"

"I don't own the place, but I'm one of the managers," Seth said. "Just so happened to be my shift last night so, even though the owner was here, I'm the one that has to deal with the fallout of all of this. Sorry. He's working tomorrow if you want to talk to him. I'm not trying to get out of it, just figured he's going to be of more help."

"Nothing to apologise for," Kidd said. "Just not ideal, that's all. Zoe will be working this case."

"Oh."

"Yes," Kidd said. He needed to keep on task, get back to the matter at hand. It didn't matter that Zoe would be on the team investigating this. Seth, as far as they knew, hadn't done anything wrong. And so long as he remained cooperative, then they weren't going to have any problems.

"Well, the owner's name is Lawrence Brewer," Seth said. "Brewer, owning a bar, almost like he was predestined." It was an attempt at a joke, a nervous attempt, Kidd could tell. He wasn't laughing. "But he's working tomorrow. I can give you his number if that would be useful."

"I think it would," Kidd said.

"What else can I do to help while I'm here?" Seth

asked. It was music to Kidd's ears. "I'm not Lawrence, but I'm probably here as often as he is, and I was on the floor last night. He was in the office."

"Can you walk me through what happened last night?" Kidd asked. "Was it a standard night?"

"Well, it was a Saturday night," Seth started. "So, as I'm sure you can imagine, it was one of our busier nights, a lot of people here, a lot of them drunk. So people line up outside, normally running right past the TK Maxx and then they come in, get searched, occasionally use the cloakroom, get a free shot, and then crack on with their night."

"A free shot. You are generous."

"Or cruel, depends on how you feel about Sambuca."

"Cruel," Kidd replied, wincing at the memory of the taste from many, many years ago. "You get many problems here?"

"We've got a pretty solid security team, so things don't normally get out of hand," Seth said. "Owner is pretty clear on not wanting people to be completely hammered when they come in, so we turn a lot of people away. Not worth ruining everyone's night for the sake of one idiot. He's good for that, at least."

"But not for other things?"

"He's a businessman. He still needs to make his money," Seth replied. "Morris and Betty were on last night. Christ, it sounds like a double act, but they were working the door. I can give you their numbers, see if they saw anything suspicious."

"That would be very helpful," Kidd said. He already liked where this was going. In case he wasn't already a fan of Seth for making Zoe so happy, this just about sealed the deal. He seemed like a decent enough guy, at least as far as Kidd was concerned at this point. "We're going to need to take a look at your CCTV," Kidd continued. "I know you've likely got a lot of cameras in here and an awful lot of footage we can comb through, but anything with our victim in it could be useful to us."

"I've already started," Seth said. Kidd blinked. "Sorry, wasn't trying to be a goody-goody or anything but... I saw the body before... well... before you got here and I... I thought I would try and make myself useful."

Kidd's heart was already pounding out of his chest. It felt like Seth was about to deliver him something major. He watched as Seth went into the room behind the bar and came back holding a small handbag.

"Then you might want to take a look at this," Seth said, putting the purse on the counter. He opened it up, taking out a wallet and a stack of twenty-pound notes held together by an elastic band.

"Holy shit," Kidd breathed.

CHAPTER
SIX

Nina Hawkins. Twenty-two years old.

"It was in the lost and found," Seth said. "It was the only thing left in there at the end of the night, so I took a little look inside, gloves on of course, and... well... that's her, isn't it?"

"Yes," Kidd replied. "That's her."

INSIDE THE PURSE, ALONG WITH THE STACK OF CASH, was a bank card and a driver's license, with a clear photo of Nina and her address. The purse gave them a very clear heading. It gave them an address, it gave them a name, and it wouldn't be too long before they had multiple addresses to investigate.

It turned out she lived in Kingston, but her family lived out in Epsom, quite a way away.

They got in touch with the family as quickly as possible, their first port of call, knowing that they would need them to identify the body. The picture on her license matched her face perfectly, but once it was confirmed that their victim was Nina Hawkins, things would become clearer still. They had things they needed to work towards.

Kidd got the cash bagged up and sent it away for testing. He wasn't sure what he was looking for on something like that, but fingerprints could lead them somewhere, or even traces of drugs that could link it to another case. The thought of it having anything to do with drugs made his blood run cold. He associated it so much with Andrea that it made him uncomfortable, like she was watching, like she was always looking over his shoulder.

There was every possibility that, even if there were traces of drugs found on the cash, it would have nothing to do with her. Drugs were in Kingston before Andrea, they would be there afterwards, but it still didn't sit right with him.

DC Powell had been setting up the big board since they got back to the station, Kidd and the rest of the team establishing contact with the pathologist, with the local council, with anyone who might be able to give them information on her last movements. He tasked Ash to check her out online, see what they could find out about her.

The rest of Kidd's conversation with Seth had

been pretty useful. Kidd had thanked Seth and asked him to chase up the CCTV as quickly as possible. He didn't have full access to it, that being something that only Lawrence Brewer was going to be able to get them, but he was going to make sure to chase him on it. Kidd was grateful to have him onside.

Kidd anticipated a second visit to The Snake Pit in the future. Based on the way Seth was talking about his boss, he couldn't imagine he was going to be the most useful person. The one thing Kidd thought was that if they were ID-checking everyone who went into that club, they would have a list of people that they could get in contact with, especially if they were seen anywhere near Nina. They stored that information, he knew that much. So, one way or another, they had a list of suspects.

It'll be a list some five hundred people long, but still, Kidd thought.

This was the part where they would likely gather their leads, where things would steadily start to become clearer. But no matter how many times Kidd did this, it never got any easier. He had to keep himself as removed as possible, try not to let himself get too hung up on how young the girl was, on the potential that was cut short. It was a tragedy.

He talked with Weaver for a little while, the DCI wanting to make sure that he felt like he was in a fit enough state to deal with all of this.

"You've just got back," Weaver said. "I know it's

your job, and I know you've been dealing with stuff down in Southend, but this is a lot to be going into when you've barely set foot in the door."

Kidd considered it for a moment, genuinely asking himself if it might be too much. He was trying to be better, broadly speaking. When he'd been in Kingston previously, he'd become overwhelmed. That was what had led to him leaving, to take a sabbatical. But in a lot of ways, it was better for him to stay busy, better for his brain to be put to use rather than sitting there and waiting.

"I'll be grand," he replied. "But I'll be sure to keep you posted if that changes. Any support you can offer would be greatly appreciated."

He didn't necessarily have a lot of faith that there would be huge amounts of support from DCI Weaver, it was a rare day that he got his hands dirty. Besides, they had a full complement on a team now, so there wasn't really any reason for him to be involved. But Weaver was making an effort to make sure Kidd was alright, there was no reason for him not to cash in on that.

"Who did you speak to at The Snake Pit?" Zoe asked.

Kidd raised an eyebrow. "I finally met the man you've been talking to me about on the phone for all of these weeks," Kidd said. "He seems nice."

"He is nice."

"He's been very helpful. He's got the initial CCTV,

and gave us the handbag from the lost and found, which got us the ID," Kidd said. "He's checking through everything else now, and he's going to get it all sent over so that Powell can take a good long look at it."

"My eyes are going to go square!" Powell called, looking over from the big board.

"It's for a good cause," Kidd called back.

Zoe hovered a little, suddenly nervous. "What did you think of him?"

Kidd blinked. "What?"

"Of Seth. What did you think of Seth?"

"It wasn't a social call," Kidd said with a chuckle. "He seemed perfectly nice. I'd love to get to know him better, maybe when we're not dealing with a dead body or something."

"Yeah, that might be an idea," Sanchez said.

"You weren't looking for my approval, were you?" Kidd asked, tentatively.

She didn't need his approval for anything. A few months ago, she was dating Owen Campbell, and if she'd asked him about that, he absolutely wouldn't have approved because Campbell, God rest his soul, had been a bit of a twat. But if she liked him, that was all that mattered. Same with Seth. His opinion didn't matter.

"Just curious," she said.

Kidd gathered the information that they had so far and relayed it to the rest of the team, steadily forming the beginnings of a game plan in his head. They would need to split up, cover as much ground as possible, and while DC Powell was gathering information on Nina from the Internet, they would be gathering it from those who knew her best. It would all add up to a bigger picture, one that would hopefully lead them to question the right people.

"You want us to split up?" Janya suggested when Kidd relayed the information to them. She had read his mind. "Happy to go with DC Hale to either one of the addresses, just let us know which."

"Thank you, Janya," Kidd replied. "If you could go to her flat, that would be great. If there are any roommates, discuss things with them, and get a sense of what her life was like. See if you can find any indication as to why the hell she was carrying that amount of cash around. Zoe and I will go and chat with the parents after they've identified the body."

"Family Liaison at Surrey Police will be in touch ASAP," Powell piped up from his desk. "They're all trying to get the gossip from me about DI McMichaels..." He paused. "I guess I shouldn't call him that anymore. Vince. That feels weird."

It took Kidd a moment to remember that DI McMichaels had worked at Surrey Police before he'd joined The Met, before he'd taken over his job for a little while. And the mention of FLOs, suddenly had him thinking of Caitlyn Jones. He'd known her for a number of years, and it was her brother who had joined the team and ultimately found himself wrapped up in organised crime with Andrea Peyton and the former DI, Vince McMichaels. He wondered if Caitlyn was taking a bit of time off to process all of that.

After Owen had been killed, Kidd had done the same. He didn't want people looking at him differently, didn't want people questioning him about what had happened. He hoped she was doing the same thing. It could be hard enough to be here without people whispering behind your back, watching your every move. He made a mental note to reach out to her, to make sure she was okay. She might not want to talk to him about it or anything, but it was always good to know that there were people in your corner.

"I'm going to stay on The Snake Pit," Powell said. "That CCTV is going to be essential for finding out who she went to the club with."

"And who she left with," Kidd added. "Let's get moving. Report back as and when. Let's see what we can get."

CHAPTER
SEVEN

The drive to Epsom took a little longer than either of them had expected. Once Nina's parents had been to identify the body, and had been paired up with a Family Liaison Officer from Surrey Police. They would likely be looking after them, despite this being a case for The Met. They didn't get to work together all that often, but it made sense for someone in the local area to be taking care of them.

The drive was pleasant enough, out of the slightly more hustle and bustle area of Kingston and into the depths of Surrey, where things were a little greener and the houses were a lot bigger, the driveways more pronounced, the cars 4x4s with the ability to go off-road despite the fact that everything was kept so perfectly. When on earth would they have the opportunity to go off-road?

"Toto, I don't think we're in Kansas anymore,"

Zoe muttered as they pulled up outside the address. The house was magnificent. Red brick that looked like it had been freshly jet washed, the most perfectly manicured front garden Kidd had ever seen, and a door that looked more like something you'd find in Hobbiton than Epsom. It was wooden and round, with a shiny gold knocker in the middle of it. Everything about it looked like it was dripping money, and Kidd could feel himself getting more uncomfortable with every passing second. It was things like this that gave him class anxiety, made him look at his shoes, and try to remember the last time he'd polished them.

"Not what I was expecting," Kidd said. "Probably should have looked at it on Google Earth before we came."

"Why? Would you have dressed nicer?"

She had him pegged, and Kidd kind of hated it.

"You know how these houses and these kinds of people make me feel," Kidd replied.

"So you're judging them based on them having a nice house?"

"Absolutely, I am," he quipped in response. "Come on, let's see what they have to say for themselves."

They made their way to the front door, Kidd hammering the shiny gold knocker and listening to the steady boom of it echoing through the house beyond. It's possible he imagined that second part, but it just felt like the kind of thing that would happen when you banged on a door quite this heavy.

The door slowly creaked open, revealing a man standing in it. He was tall, which was the first thing Kidd noticed about him. Tall, broad, and staring down at the two detectives like they had just interrupted something incredibly important.

"Can I help you?" The voice was exactly the one that Kidd had been expecting, smooth, silky, posh, so posh that it almost sounded like it hurt him to speak to anyone.

"My name is Detective Inspector Benjamin Kidd," Kidd started, doing his best to keep his voice level and clear. "This is my colleague, Detective Sergeant Zoe Sanchez. We're here to discuss Nina Hawkins. Are Mr and Mrs Hawkins in?"

The door opened fully, the tall, broad man now revealing his full height, his full breadth, because he was built like an Olympian. No wonder the door needed to be so large; he filled it out so well that a normal door frame simply wouldn't do.

"I am Mr Hawkins," he said, voice still silky smooth, though perhaps now with a slight edge to it. "Joshua Hawkins." He brought a meaty hand to his face, rubbing his eyes. He looked exhausted. It had likely been one hell of a day for Mr Hawkins. "Sorry, it's been a difficult few hours. I feel like we'd barely sat down and... here you are."

"Mrs Hawkins is inside?"

"She's just popped out to get some food," he said. "We... we didn't have anything in. At least, nothing that she wanted to eat or drink, and she just..." He ran his hand through his hair. "I think she just wanted to get away from me. It's been.... It's been a very difficult day." He finally looked at the two detectives again and forced a smile. "You don't care about any of that. Sorry. Would you like to come inside and wait for her? Would you like some tea?"

"If you wouldn't mind," Kidd replied.

Joshua gestured for them to enter, the door closing behind them with a heavy slam, a sense of finality accompanying the banishing of the outside chill. He guided them through an opulent hallway with gilded wallpaper, and art hung in frames where perhaps photographs of the family would have been in an average family home.

Kidd followed, taking everything in with interest, noting how clean and tidy everything was, how well put together the house was, the detail in all the decoration. It wasn't necessarily pertinent to the case, but it was always interesting to see how the other half lived.

Mr Hawkins took them through to the kitchen, which was starkly modern in contrast to the entryway. There were black marble countertops, cupboards that didn't appear to have handles, and large, panoramic windows that showed off the grounds. That's how you knew a house was posh, when it stopped being a garden and became "grounds."

The dining room table had plates on it with half-eaten food, a coffee pot that still had half the coffee left in it. The knives and forks were haphazardly left on the table, a newspaper open in front of one of the plates. This was where they'd been when they'd received the call about their daughter. Their lives had frozen in that moment. They'd not returned to it. How could they?

"I'm so sorry," Joshua said, quickly clearing the plates, the coffee pot, the cups. He wiped down the table before offering them seats, moving back to the kitchen and putting on the kettle. The door opened and closed as he poured hot water into the cups.

A woman walked into the kitchen, a tote bag in one hand, her black handbag hanging limply in the other. When she caught sight of the detectives, she stopped dead, staring at the two of them like they were intruders in her home.

"Vivian, this is Detective Inspector Benjamin Kidd and Detective Constable Zoe Sanchez," Joshua said. "They're here to talk about Nina."

"Good," she said, turning her focus to her husband. "Are you making tea?"

"Yes," Joshua said. "Would you like one?"

"Please."

There was a coldness to the room. The whiteness of the walls with the black countertops and the grey

49

cupboards, the cold light of the midmorning pouring through the windows, no lights on, not even a lamp. Everything was bathed in a haze of grey, which, given the news they had been met with that morning, wasn't altogether surprising.

Joshua made them tea and joined them at the dining table, where the two detectives took a seat opposite the grieving parents. There was a silence, a hush that seemed to spread to the deepest corners of the house. Was it always like this? Or was it just the recent news that had caused things to be this way?

"Thank you for seeing us on such short notice," Kidd said. "I'm sure you understand that with investigations like this, time is of the essence. The more information we can get at this early stage, the more likely we are to be successful in solving it."

"Solving the murder of our daughter," Vivian said, like she was trying it on, seeing how it sounded to say something like that aloud.

"Yes," Kidd replied. "I'm terribly sorry for your loss."

"Your sorrow means nothing," she said, taking a sip of her tea. "But I appreciate it, nevertheless."

"We wanted to ask you a few questions about Nina," Kidd said. "We want to get a sense of the life she was living, anyone she might have known, places of interest that we can look into. Would that be alright?"

Vivian looked at Kidd blankly, like he'd just

spoken to her in a foreign language. She wasn't happy that they were there, and no amount of him treading carefully around the situation seemed to help what she was feeling in that moment. He'd dealt with his fair share of upset victims before; it wasn't his first rodeo. He just hoped she'd be able to help them somewhat.

"We... We don't know." Vivian seemed standoff-ish, embarrassed almost to be revealing this information to Kidd and Zoe. Kidd needed a little more.

"What do you mean, you don't know?" He pressed. He didn't want to seem pushy, but it was all so vague, too vague, in fact.

Vivian looked over at her husband, and he looked back at her with an equally blank expression, like neither one of them truly knew how to express what they were about to say to the detective.

"We hadn't had a lot of contact with Nina over the past few years," Vivian said, apparently the one more willing to take the lead on this. Joshua seemed at a loss. "She... She had changed a lot from when she used to live at home, and those changes were not really things that the two of us agreed with."

Kidd sat up a little straight. "What kind of things?" He asked.

"She changed," Vivian said. "She became... more of a party girl. We stopped recognising who she was. She'd come back here stinking of booze, she'd be on a comedown. Who knew what else?"

The mention of a comedown sent a spike of anxiety through Kidd as he thought about the money she'd had in her purse, the history of drugs running around Kingston, the looming presence of Andrea Peyton...

"It's where all of her money was going," Vivian said. "When she was at Uni, it was her student loan, and then when she started working, it all just kept going to that. No matter what we did to try and curb that, to stop her, she seemed intent on pissing all her money down the drain. We... We couldn't take it anymore. And now... Now it's too late."

The tears started to fall now, tumbling down her face and cascading down her jawline. But she didn't make a sound. There were no theatrics; there were just tears, and somehow that seemed to strike even harder with Kidd. She couldn't stop the tears from falling, but somehow couldn't bring herself to cry out.

"Did you stop having contact with her?" Kidd asked.

Vivian nodded. "We... We told her that if that was the way she was going to behave then we didn't want anything to do with her," Vivian said. "In some ways, I think we thought that maybe it would scare her into changing. She'd realise that she was about to lose us and that would be enough to... I don't know...To stop her from acting out in that way. But..." She let the words vanish into her tea, taking a sip from the still-steaming cup. She winced a little, the heat a little too much to bear.

"When was this?" Kidd asked.

Vivian sniffed. "Best part of a year ago," she said. "She... took us at our word. There was an argument where she wanted to know if we were serious, and we doubled down, told her that we meant it and..." She swallowed, a thought striking her so hard that Kidd practically heard it make contact with the inside of her skull. "When you make an ultimatum like that, you have to stick to it. When you draw a line in the sand, you have to be certain that you aren't going to cross it. And we drew that line and have been on this side of it ever since."

Kidd couldn't help but notice how quiet Joshua was being during all of this. His hands were wrapped around his mug of tea, fingernails bitten down to nubs, knuckles white. It was a wonder the mug didn't crack under the pressure of his hulking hands.

"Mr Hawkins," Kidd said, and Joshua looked up, apparently surprised to be called on at all. "Is that what happened?"

Joshua looked at Vivian and then back at the detectives, apparently weighing up his options. It set Kidd on the edge of his seat, because not agreeing immediately that's how things had been, likely meant that Joshua Hawkins had something to hide.

"Mr Hawkins?" Kidd asked again.

"I... I saw her."

Vivian turned to him sharply.

"About... six weeks ago, I saw her," he said, voice trembling. "She wanted my help. And I turned her down."

Bingo.

CHAPTER
EIGHT

D C Janya Ravel didn't know what to expect when she made her way to Nina Hawkins' flat that morning. She was living in a house share with a couple of friends a little way outside of Kingston, and she knew that it was going to be a difficult conversation when she stepped through those doors, but she hadn't expected two people who were very much on the verge of falling to pieces.

"You're fucking kidding." Paige New was the girl who had answered the door, the one who thought they were coming to ask questions about Nina, not to tell them that she was dead. She could barely get the words out, sitting on a cream sofa that had several splits in the leather.

She was still in her pyjamas, a white strappy top and a pair of baggy shorts that hit her mid-thigh, fake tanned legs that seemed to go on forever, cut off by fluffy slipper socks. Her bleach-blonde hair was piled high on top of her head, strands of it sticking out at odd angles, clearly pulled up in a hurry.

They were in the open-plan living/dining/kitchen area, the sofa pushed up against the wall facing a TV that looked almost brand new. It was comically big, far too big to be able to comfortably sit and watch something without getting some kind of neck pain.

The flat was clean, tidy for the most part, but for the table, which was covered in a graveyard of empty glass bottles, white wine, Prosecco, bottles of beer, cider, even a couple of glass bottles of Coke. It was a clear sign to Janya that they'd been living the high life. Who on earth had glass bottles of Coke outside of a restaurant, except for the aesthetic?

They'd clearly been getting on it the night before in a pretty big way, which would explain why they had found Nina near The Snake Pit. This was the aftermath of their pre-drinks, and what an aftermath it was. It was an obscene amount of alcohol. Surely, it hadn't just been the three girls? How Paige was even managing to stay upright seemed miraculous.

Janya sniffed. There was alcohol in the air, floating around like she could get some kind of contact high if she breathed in a little too deeply. She looked over to the kitchen and could see the take-away boxes stacked on the counter, yellow polystyrene that made her teeth itch at the thought of them scraping across one another.

While they'd been concerned about Nina this morning, their concerns hadn't been there last night. They'd come back and had their drunken kebabs, and only realised she wasn't there this morning. Or perhaps when she didn't respond to their messages.

Did Nina disappear on a night out often? Was she one of those friends who had these crazy adventures that she would regale them with when the morning rolled around and she stumbled back through the door?

Nina had two roommates. There was Paige who had answered the door, and Sienna Parks, who had yet to sit down. She looked a lot more put together than Paige, like maybe she'd been up for longer, had enough time to straighten her brunette hair so it fell like a river down her back. She kept pacing back and forth, wearing a track into the obsessively clean carpet. She was also in her pyjamas, or at least they looked like pyjamas. Janya couldn't be sure. Jogging bottoms and a t-shirt that looked like it desperately needed to be reintroduced to the washing machine.

"Tea?" Sienna said suddenly. "Do you want tea? We could make tea?"

Janya offered her a gentle smile. She was stressed, that much she could see. She was just trying to help.

"Sure thing," Janya said, turning to Ash. "Ash? Tea?"

"Please," he said. "Just milk for me."

"Milk, two sugars," Janya said. "Thank you, Sienna."

They waited for Sienna to make the tea, the kettle taking what felt like an age to boil, leaving them sitting there waiting in relative silence.

Once they'd been presented with cups of tea that looked like their relationship with the teabag had been nothing more than a passing acquaintance, Janya decided to get down to business, and silently decided that the tea would remain untouched.

"I'm sorry to be coming here with such bleak news," Janya said. "Had you already called the police this morning?"

"I did, yes," Paige said, earning herself a sharp glance from Sienna. Something Janya made a mental note to dig into later on. "Nina... Nina has always been a bit of a wild card, we didn't know where she would end up on a night out. She loved to find the next place and the next place so her not being home wasn't a... It wasn't really a worry."

"So you happily came home without her last night?" Janya asked.

"I wouldn't say happily," Paige said, her voice a little meek, a little mousy. She felt like she was being led into a trap. Janya didn't want to do that to her, but she wasn't overly impressed with them not looking out for one another. "But it was how she did things, and so we dropped her a message as we normally do and told her we were on our way home. That there's... There's a kebab for her in the fridge." Paige sniffed, tears were incoming. "She would heat it up when she got in, microwave it or something. She always said it was better that way, but..." The tears came now, full force, running down her face.

Janya picked up a box of tissues from the shelf beneath the table. It had clearly been shoved aside in favour of the alcohol. She handed it to Paige, who blew her nose at a deafening volume.

"I called the police this morning because she would always reply to a message," Paige said. "And then she wasn't picking up her phone either, so I figured... I don't know, I figured something must have gone wrong. I thought you were the right people to turn to."

"You did the right thing," Janya said, clocking a small eye roll from Sienna. Maybe it was time to quiz the other housemate. "Do you want to tell us a little more about Nina, Sienna?" Janya added.

Sienna seemed surprised to be called upon, like her presence was purely ceremonial. "What?"

"I think Paige needs a bit of time to compose herself," Janya said, nodding to Paige, who was pulling out a second and third tissue to fix herself up. "Let's give her that time while you tell me about Nina."

"What do you want to know?"

"What do you think is worth us knowing?" Janya asked. "You three lived here together?"

"Yes," she replied. "There's another housemate too, Bailey, but she's away right now, so she didn't go out with us."

"Where is she?"

"At home with her family in Essex."

"So, do you go out together often?" Janya asked.

"A fair amount," she said. "We all work pretty hard, so we're just trying to blow off steam when we can."

"What do you do?"

"I'm a teaching assistant, Paige works for a publisher in London, Nina manages a clothes shop in town, and Bailey works in bars. It's a lot of work just trying to get by, so... so when we have a bit of spare money, or enough money to treat ourselves, we go on a night out."

"The pre-drinking looks pretty serious," Ash said with a smirk.

"When you're totally broke, you have to make the pre- serious," Sienna said with a smirk. "That's one thing we all took from Uni and never really let go of. You know how to squeeze every penny out of a night out, and showing up three sheets to the wind is sometimes the best way to do that."

"Certainly a cheaper night out," Janya said.

"Exactly."

"So you're all struggling for money?" Janya added.

Sienna blinked. "What's that?"

"You're struggling for money," she repeated. "You said that you have to make the pre- serious when you're broke, so you're broke?"

Sienna swallowed, like she'd maybe said a little bit too much. Now it felt like she was getting somewhere, like tugging at this thread might make the whole outfit unravel.

"We are," Sienna said. "Some more than most, but that doesn't mean we don't want to have a good time when we can."

"How are Nina's finances?"

Paige said, "Awful," at the same time Sienna said, "Fine."

What was Sienna trying to hide? What was she keeping from them? Why did she want to keep their lack of funds a secret? There was something in it, Janya just knew it.

"There's always a lot of month left at the end of the money," Sienna said. "It wasn't an all-the-time thing, just when it got closer to payday, things got a bit tight. Nina was never very good at budgeting."

"She doesn't get paid as much as we do," Paige said. "I mean, a publishing salary isn't the best, neither is a teaching one, but it's a salary. Nina isn't on too much more than minimum wage, so... So payday always meant more to her than the rest of us."

"But you all struggle?"

"Sometimes," Paige said. "But who doesn't?

Everything is getting more expensive. It's hard to live even a semi-decent life at the moment because everything is so expensive and prices just keep on going up and up."

"Fair enough," Janya said. She'd felt the pinch herself, but still couldn't help but feel like there was something that wasn't coming her way, something they were intentionally trying to keep from her. "Is there anything you can tell us about Nina that you think might be useful?" Janya asked. "Any unusual behaviour or people she might be connected to that could be of use to us?"

They looked at one another, the two of them thinking it through. Paige fidgeted, turning back to the detectives.

"What do you mean by that?"

Janya thought back to what Kidd had told them about the body by the river, the way it had been left there, the way it seemed to be sending a message. It was possible that these girls might be able to give them some idea of who their killer was trying to send a message to.

"Just curious as to other leads we might be able to follow," Janya said. "Murder is rarely a random thing. It is much more likely to be someone the victim knows, or someone they are associated with. So, is there anything that has been happening in Nina's life recently that might point to her being in some kind of trouble?"

There was another pause, but they didn't look at one another this time. Instead, they stuck to their own brains as they tried to figure out exactly what could have been going on. Maybe Janya had read the situation wrong, maybe they weren't as clued in on Nina's personal life as she had thought, as she had hoped.

Sienna spoke up first. "I can't think of anything," she said. "It might be worth talking to the people she worked with. Maybe they know something more. She told us most things."

"Most things?"

"Well, everybody has secrets, right?" Sienna said.

And there it was again, that hint that Sienna knew more than she was letting on. Janya just couldn't prove it, nor could she find the right question to ask to get Sienna to start talking. She turned her attention to Paige.

"Sienna's right," Paige said. "People she worked with might be useful. They might know more than we do."

"Anyone in particular you think we should talk to?" Janya asked.

They looked at one another, almost like neither one of them wanted to say who they were thinking about. This lack of information was starting to become tiring.

"Please?" Janya added.

"There was someone she worked with, another

manager called Blake Glover," Paige said. "He... He showed up on the night out."

"What is her relationship with Blake like?"

"Not particularly good," Paige said.

"Paige."

"What, Sienna? It's not!" Paige snapped. "He was there last night. They had a bit of a fight because he fancies her or something, but Nina just wasn't interested. I don't know if... I don't know if that's something to go off of."

Ash wrote it down, and Janya found herself nodding. It would certainly be a start.

"Thank you," she said. "Do you mind if we take a quick look around Nina's bedroom? Just see if we can see anything that might help us."

There was a slight hesitation, but they agreed, and Paige was the one who showed Janya and Ash upstairs to Nina's bedroom. It was sparkling clean, like she'd maybe tidied it before she'd left for the night out. Janya cast her mind back to when she used to go on nights out, how there would always be clothes on the bed that she'd discarded, ones she'd decided she wasn't going to wear. This was like a totally different world.

"Well, they're an interesting pair," Ash said quietly.

"What do you mean?"

"They can't seem to decide what the right thing is

to say to you," Ash said. "It's like they're hiding things."

"Glad we're on the same page, DC Hale. I think they're hiding plenty of things," Janya said. "That's why we're here. Because Nina can't hide a damn thing from us."

They started looking through the drawers of the desk, the bedside table, anything that was a potential hiding place. Would they come across more money? Would they come across something that could point them to where all that cash had come from? Maybe. It was possible.

"You find anything?" Janya asked Ash.

He'd been looking over the desk. It was probably the least tidy place in the entire bedroom, a couple of wayward pieces of paper, a mug of tea that looked like it had been drunk the previous day, the dregs of it still hanging around in the bottom of it, around the rim.

"Maybe," Ash said, pulling something out of the drawer. It was a bundle of papers in a plastic folder, hand-written notes. "Jesus Christ."

"What?" Janya asked, giving him her undivided attention.

"I've definitely found something," he said, handing the papers to Janya. "Someone was threatening Nina."

CHAPTER
NINE

"What on earth are you talking about?" Vivian snapped, her voice sharp. The temperature in the room had gone down a few degrees. "You didn't tell me about this."

"Vivian—"

"No," she interrupted. "You didn't tell me that our daughter had been in touch, and now she's dead, so I need you to tell me why on earth you didn't tell me?"

"I didn't... I didn't think that..." Joshua looked to Kidd like he was about to jump in and help, but he had no intention of derailing this. What Joshua had revealed was important. The conversation they were having was telling, not just about their relationship with each other, but with their daughter. He wanted to let this play out. "We should discuss this later."

"We should discuss this right now," Vivian snapped. "You saw our daughter, she came to you, and you didn't think to tell me. How is that fair? I've not seen her in more than a year because of what we said, because of what we agreed, and now I find out that you are the one who got to see our daughter before she died, you are the one who got to have last words with her?"

"Vivian, not now."

"No time like the present," she said, her eyes wide, staring in disbelief at her husband. "What do you have to say for yourself? Because I can't see a single excuse you could possibly make that will make any of this better."

"Then why are you asking for one and making a scene?" Joshua said.

It was such a cold response, Kidd practically felt the breath being knocked out of him, so how would Vivian be feeling in that moment?

A tense silence fell. Kidd watched as Vivian weighed up her options. She fixed a soft sort of smile onto her face as she turned her attention back to Kidd and Zoe.

"I can't stand this," she said, looking at the two detectives in turn. "I'm sorry, I think you have more to discuss with my husband than you do with me."

"Vivian—"

"Don't," she interrupted. "I can't even look at you right now. Don't follow me."

Vivian got to her feet, and crossed to the kitchen door. She left the room, slamming the door behind her. Kidd practically felt the walls shake. Kidd still expected Joshua to try and follow her, try and reason with her, but he just stayed in his seat, eyes fixed on the table.

"That could have gone better," Joshua muttered. Kidd wanted to make a comment, something snide to drive the knife in, but what would be the point? He still needed information out of Joshua, regardless of how he felt about him.

"Do you want to tell us what happened, Mr Hawkins?" Kidd asked.

Joshua sighed, looking towards the door like he was considering going after Vivian, but he quickly seemed to change his mind.

"It wasn't a happy conversation," he said. "She had come to me looking for more money, she was in... She was in a pretty bad way financially, wasn't sure she was going to make it to her next payday, and she... She was deeply in debt."

"In debt?"

"Maxed out overdraft, credit cards, that kind of thing," Joshua said. "She was desperate, which I think was why she'd reached out to me in the first place after she'd spent such a long time not reaching out at all. It had been radio silence up until that point. She needed me and I... I turned her away."

Kidd was shocked at that, half expecting it to be Joshua who had given her that big stack of money, but no. So where had that money come from? Why was she carrying it around with her? And why hadn't she used it to pay off her debt yet?

"You turned her away?"

"I didn't want to," Joshua said quickly. "All I could think of in that moment was what Vivian and I had decided, the discussion we'd had to hold the line, to wait until Nina changed so that we could help her, but it just... It didn't seem like she'd changed. I was going to tell Vivian about it, but I thought... I thought she'd be upset." He scoffed. "Imagine that."

"Well, I'd say you keeping it from her is probably what prompted that reaction," Zoe said. "Especially given that your daughter is now dead, and you had seen her fairly recently."

"I know why she reacted that way, I'm not stupid," Joshua snapped. "But it wasn't like I reached out to her behind Vivian's back, it wasn't like I was trying to make contact with her again, she came to me and asked for my help, and I told her that I couldn't do that. So... So I sent her on her way and..." He shook his head. "If that's why she was killed, then I don't know what I'll do with myself."

"What do you mean by that?" Kidd asked, even though he knew quite well exactly what he meant.

"People do stupid things when they are in debt, Detective," Joshua said. "She tried to tell me that she needed help, but wouldn't tell me the kind of trouble she was in, or how bad it was, no matter how hard I asked, no matter how hard I pressed. I guess what

I'm saying is, I'm worried she's done something stupid and... and me not helping her has... resulted in these consequences."

A far-off look fell across his eyes. No doubt he was thinking about how Nina had met her end, the circumstances, the reasons. There was every possibility that Joshua was right, that Nina had got herself into the kind of trouble where this was the only outcome. He didn't want it to be true, but there were so many signs. Kidd had a bad feeling about this, a very bad feeling indeed.

Kidd was silent as they left the house, and got in the car. Neither one of them knew what to say, and Kidd couldn't help but wonder if they were having the same thoughts—if Zoe was aboard the same train as him, running towards the conclusion that Andrea would be at the centre of this again.

So, when people were short of money, they ended up working for her. It was what had happened with Craig all those years ago, and Zoe had seen it happen in her own cases while Kidd had been away. He wasn't sure what to do. He didn't know if he could go through another case where he was dancing through the traps as Andrea was setting them.

"We're both thinking the same thing, aren't we?" Zoe said.

"I don't want that to be true," Kidd said. "And I'm not entirely sure how I'm supposed to go about finding out. It's a door that I was hoping would stay closed, especially now that Organised Crime has been all over it since that case you had."

"I've not received any updates on it recently," Zoe said. "Out of sight, out of mind."

"Yeah," Kidd said, starting the car. "What did you think of the pair of them?"

"Did you have Dysfunctional Family on your bingo card?" Zoe asked. "Because I didn't, not this time around. I thought... I don't know what I thought. It just kept getting worse. They'd drifted apart and..."

"Dad really did want to help," Kidd said. "But was so determined to do right by his wife that now he'll likely regret not doing right by his daughter for the rest of his life."

"He's bound to," Zoe said. "I'm not saying it's his fault, but... I don't know, chain reactions and all that. One thing leads to another."

"Agreed," Kidd said.

They'd managed to get Vivian to come back into the room after they'd finished speaking to Joshua. They'd not wanted to leave them with things being how they were, but needs must. They had a case to investigate, and they couldn't be babysitting two grownups.

"We need to make sure a FLO gets to them as

soon as possible. They can't be left alone to rattle around that big house," Zoe said, looking out of the window as they drove. "I can't begin to tell you how much I hate that you're driving."

"Shut up."

"You never used to drive, and I hate it when you do," she said, hanging on a little tighter to her seat belt. "Have you ever been to The Snake Pit before this morning?"

Kidd snorted. "Never," he said. "Used to walk past it every morning. It's on the way to work if I want to walk by the river. Think I'm maybe a little too old for clubs. We'll need to talk to the bouncers who were working there last night, see if they saw anything. I wonder how Janya is getting on."

"Hopefully keeping things moving forward," Zoe said. "Seriously, you're never driving again. I hate this."

Things were opening up, every path they took leading them somewhere new, to something else, to someone else. They just needed to keep following them, and not get lost along the way.

CHAPTER
TEN

T hey got back to the station in pretty good time, waiting for Janya and Ash to show up before they debriefed the rest of the team. Powell had been hard at work on the evidence board, despite the minimal amount of evidence they had so far, updating with whatever information he'd managed to gather about Nina from the internet, place of work, network of friends, that kind of thing.

While they were waiting, Kidd put in a call to Lawrence Brewer at The Snake Pit. It took him a couple of tries before he got through.

"You're the one investigating what happened outside my club, then?" Lawrence's voice was a little rough, like he survived on a diet of cigarettes and whiskey. "What are you going to do about it?"

"We're investigating it," Kidd said, not enjoying the man's attitude. He was clearly going to be an absolute joy to speak to. "I'd love to come in and chat to you about the happenings in your club, if that's alright? I assume you'll have access to the CCTV."

"We're working on that," Lawrence said. "You spoke to one of my managers, Seth. He's been getting at me about it all day."

"Glad to hear it."

"Hmmm." Lawrence apparently wasn't too happy about that. "I'll be there all day tomorrow. Come and talk to me then."

"Today doesn't work for you?"

"I'm a very busy man."

"Too busy to discuss a murder that happened outside your club?"

"Don't twist my words, Detective, I wouldn't want us getting off on the wrong foot."

Kidd allowed that to hang in the air, allowing Lawrence to realise that he had pretty much just threatened a police officer.

"Sorry," he blurted. "It's been a long day."

"Agreed," Kidd replied. "I'll see you tomorrow, Mr Brewer."

Kidd hung up the phone and turned his attention to Zoe.

"So he sounds like a prick," she said.

"You have such a way with words, Sanchez."

"What can I say?" She replied. "I'm gifted."

Janya and Ash showed up not too long after Kidd hung up the phone, Powell then taking his moment to go through the evidence board, telling them all what he'd managed to figure out about Nina Hawkins so far. He had gone quite deep on the research. It was good to see it so full, so early on.

"That's where we need to be going first," Janya said, noticing that Powell had put Perkins on the board, a small clothes shop in Kingston. "It was the only real thing we managed to get out of the two housemates."

"I've got three housemates," Powell said from his desk. "Paige, Sienna, and Bailey."

"Bailey is out of town," Janya replied.

"Worth talking to when she comes back?"

"Almost certainly," Janya said. "And then we got these." Janya handed the pieces of paper in the plastic folder to Kidd, the handwritten notes, the threats on Nina's life.

"Jesus Christ," he breathed. "Where did these come from?"

"Nina's room, in her desk drawer," Ash said. "They were just sitting there, under a couple of phone bills."

"Pretty easy find?" Kidd asked.

"Yeah, now you mention it," Ash said. "But someone was clearly upset with Nina; whoever wrote those said they were going to kill her."

"Was there anything else? It would be asking too much for these to be signed with a name and address, wouldn't it?"

"You expecting an SAE or something, boss?" Zoe quipped.

"If only."

"There's something else going on there, too," Janya said. "Something that I just can't put my finger on."

"How so?" Kidd asked.

"There was a lot of talk about money, which they then seemed to clam up about the second I started to ask a little more," Janya said. "I don't know. Sienna seems to be the one who is ruling the roost there, and I get the distinct impression that Paige isn't about to cross that line."

"You think Sienna is hiding something?"

"I do," Janya replied. "But I don't know what, and I don't know why. Their friend is dead, for crying out loud. Surely whatever it is that's going on, they're going to want this to be solved?"

"Is there a boyfriend or something? Someone else we can talk to?"

"Not as far as we know," Janya said. "But there was someone at her place of work who was interested in her. Blake Glover."

"And who is he?"

"Someone she worked with. Apparently, they had a bit of a falling out at the club last night," Janya said. "Might not be anything, but also might be something. He was interested in her, she didn't feel the same way."

"We'll get onto Perkins, then," Kidd said. "See if we can't have a little chat with Mr Glover. Good work, both of you."

"How did it go for you?" Ash asked.

"Parents haven't had contact with her for the past year because of, you guessed it, money worries," Kidd said. "She'd been living beyond her means, partying, that kind of thing. They didn't approve."

"Dad had some contact," Zoe said. "She came to him asking for money about six weeks ago, but he didn't cave."

"Bloody hell," Ash said. "So he's a bit of a hard arse?"

"Quite the opposite," Kidd said. "I think he really wanted to help, but her mum, Vivian, seemed to be determined to play hardball with Nina until she decided to turn her life around. And now she's dead."

"Shit," Ash breathed. "That's... That's bleak."

"Welcome to the job, DC Hale," Kidd replied. "Board is looking good so far, Powell. We need to keep on this, get it updated. How are we getting on with CCTV?"

"I'm on at the council and those local businesses about the CCTV," Powell replied.

"Good stuff," Kidd said. He was feeling positive, absolutely bouncy with what they'd managed to uncover so far. It wasn't that they had leads, that they knew where they were going, but moves were being made, and that was certainly something.

He made his way over to his desk and saw that there was already an article posted online about what had happened down by the river and lo-and-behold Joe Warrington was the one who'd got hold of it. It was always going to be him.

"Jesus Christ," Kidd grumbled as he read through the article. Somehow he'd managed to get the name of the victim, and in getting the name of the victim had managed to pre-empt any control they had over the information they were giving out. All it would take was a Google search, and people could now find out everything that they knew about Nina Hawkins. That happy feeling had very quickly vanished.

"What's happened?" Zoe asked.

"Joe Warrington has posted a bloody article about the victim. He's not got the proper details yet, just that she was killed by the river," Kidd growled. "Did anyone speak to the press this morning? I'm not going to tear you a new arsehole, I just need to know."

A series of frightened expressions and head shakes came back to him. It would almost be easier if it had been one of his team members who'd said the wrong thing to the wrong person. This meant that someone in the building had mentioned something, or that it had gotten out some other way.

"I'll need to talk to Weaver about it," Kidd groaned. "He's going to absolutely lose his shit over this. He hates leaks."

"You're loving this, aren't you?" Zoe said, hovering beside his desk. "You're in your element."

"I'm sorry, how did we get from me wanting to wring Joe Warrington's neck to me enjoying this?"

"Because you secretly love the drama," she replied. "You love having something to focus on and someone to rail at, and Joe Warrington is a good person to rail at. Believe me, I've done it."

"Want to fill me in on that?"

Zoe shrugged. "Maybe when you're next feeling low, it's a good story," she replied, a little more nervously than Kidd had anticipated. "But come on, admit it, you love this, love being back in the thick of it, back on home turf."

"Straight back in at the deep end, Zoe," he said. "You know me. I love getting my teeth stuck into something like this. And it's home turf, as you put it. It was one thing to be doing all this stuff in Southend, but doing it back home? I don't know, there's a buzz about it."

"You're so cracked," she said with a laugh.

"I'm going to go and chat to Weaver. Make sure he's fully up to speed with what's going on. He's going to be keeping a closer eye on me than normal, I think, I want to make sure he's up to date."

"Come back with coffee or don't come back at all," Zoe replied, heading back to her desk. "I think we're going to need it."

CHAPTER
ELEVEN

Chatting with Weaver was exactly what Kidd needed. It was nice to have the DCI on his side this time, even if he knew that once he got back into the swing of things, they would grow distant once again. Partly because Kidd had a habit of breaking the rules to get what he wanted, and partly because Weaver had a habit of not getting involved in cases if he could help it. He knew that Kidd knew what he was doing, and he didn't want to get his hands dirty.

"I've got one other thing to mention," Kidd said. "Joe Warrington has got ahead of us with press stuff."

"What?"

"Name of the victim is out there, which means we're on the back foot as far as the press goes," Kidd said. "Only going to be a matter of time before those questions from the press get really bloody specific, or before they're camping outside the parents' house trying to get information."

"Fuck's sake," Weaver groaned, dragging a hand across his face. "Just when I think that prick is going to start leaving us alone... We're going to need to set up something official then, something to keep them at bay."

"When we've got something concrete?" Kidd asked. "I've got the team on the CCTV. If we can get an image to put out, maybe we can use that as a jumping-off point, give them something to print that actually makes us look competent."

"They'll still spin it so you look like a twat."

"Sure," Kidd said. "But let's not make it easy for them."

Weaver considered it for a moment. "I'll give you as long as I can, but you know how quickly these things can snowball once they get out," he said.

"I do, boss," Kidd said. "Buy me as much time as you can."

He made his way back to the Incident Room, taking a quick coffee order from everyone before making his way to the front office, where Diane was very quick to collar him.

"You're not going to like this," she said, voice grave, lips pursed. "But I wanted to be the one to tell you because I didn't want you to get blindsided when you stepped outside the front door."

Kidd raised an eyebrow at her. Whatever this

was, it wasn't going to be good. There was no reason for Diane to be warning him about anything that was going to make his day better.

"What?" Kidd asked.

"I've been fending off the press all morning, trying to keep them at bay, telling them we will arrange something asap," she started. "But a certain someone's article has got everyone in a tizzy, and now they're waiting outside to chat to you."

"They?" Kidd asked. "Who the fuck is they?"

"Okay, first of all, you may get away with that language in your incident room, but you know I don't like it," Diane said with a raise of an eyebrow and a shake of the head. Kidd felt well and truly scolded. "They are the vultures that you so enjoy talking to, especially when ambushed. I've tried to get them to go away, but the best I've managed is getting them to get away from the steps so you can get out of here. I imagine marching orders will come a little stronger from you."

Kidd groaned. "You're joking."

"You've just got back, I wouldn't torture you with a joke like that," she said. "Do you have anything you can give them?"

"Joe Warrington has already given them something," Kidd muttered under his breath, looking past Diane and at the waiting crowd. There weren't too many of them, a couple that he recognised from local papers. It hadn't gone big yet. He could give them

85

something, at least confirm what Joe Warrington had already said, and send them on their way. He turned to Diane, forcing a smile onto his face. "I'll handle it."

"And tell them to stop calling me while you're at it," Diane said. "I'm not one to bite people's heads off, but I'll do it."

Kidd had absolutely no doubt that she would. Woe betide the person who crossed Diane.

Kidd made his way through reception and out the front doors, immediately being battered by a barrage of questions, none of them quite making their way through the noise to capture his attention. He held up his hands, trying to calm them down. They quieted.

"I'm sure you're all aware how incredibly unorthodox this is," Kidd started. "This is not an official press conference. One will be called when we have a little more information to give you. For the time being, I can confirm that the victim was Nina Hawkins, a resident of Kingston. And I want to assure you that this is being investigated by me and my team. We are looking into any and all leads related to this case. If you happen to be in possession of any such information, feel free to send it our way. Diane, or one of our other station officers, will be happy to take your call so long as you are respectful and not infringing on their time too much."

"Should people be worried about leaving their houses at night?" one of the reporters asked. Kidd recognised her as someone from the Kingston and Richmond Gazette. Her name escaped him. "Is there a killer on the loose that people should be aware of?"

"I think people need to remain calm," Kidd said. "As I said, this is an ongoing investigation, and we are keeping all of our options open and looking into all leads. I would suggest that people remain as vigilant on night outs as they always have been, make sure you're travelling in groups, make sure you know where the other members of your party are. I'm not trying to whip up any kind of frenzy here. People should be as careful as they always have been."

There was another flurry of questions: if people needed to be carrying weapons; if there was any other information that Kidd could give them so that people could stay safe; overlapping calls for more police on the streets.

"As I have said, this is an ongoing investigation," Kidd said sharply. "I don't want anyone getting too heated about all of this. When we have more information that we can share, we will hold a formal press conference. For the time being, take me at my word, we are working as quickly and efficiently as possible to make sure that this killer is brought to justice. Thank you for your time. Please get away from this police station before our station officer starts tearing you all limb from limb."

This got him a small laugh, polite, maybe a little nervous. Many of them had dealt with Diane before.

They knew what she was capable of if you happened to piss her off. No one wanted to be on her bad side.

The journalists parted, some of them making notes or speaking into their phones as they went, recording whatever they were going to publish online or in their rags the following day. Only one of them remained, and it was exactly who Kidd thought it was going to be.

"Thanks for that, Joe," Kidd said, unable to keep the venom out of his voice. "Couldn't possibly let us do this at our own pace, eh?"

Joe pulled at his beanie hat nervously, fingering the seam. It was nice to know that even after all of their dealings, Kidd still managed to find a way to make the boy nervous. They may have been on better terms than they had been at the start of their interactions, but Kidd and Joe had a history that no amount of time could heal.

It was Joe's brother, Tony, who had been responsible for the resurgence of The Grinning Murders a while back, which caused no end of bother for Kidd. It was also Tony who had been accidentally released early from prison and gone on a rampage that cost him the life of one of his officers and put another one in the hospital.

Owen Campbell was a ghost that Kidd would carry with him for the rest of his life. And he wasn't about to let Joe forget that.

"I'm a journalist," Joe said. "It's my job to break

the news when I find it, and this felt like the kind of story that my viewers deserved to know."

"Oh, they deserved to know the name of this girl before we had a chance to properly investigate her murder, did they?"

"She was killed on the borough, I think people have a right to know."

"And I think Nina had a right to a little more dignity than what you've given her," Kidd snapped. "She was a human being at the end of the day, Joe, not some piece of news fodder for your viewers. But you don't think about that, do you? You were just thinking about how many clicks that exclusive was going to get you."

"That's not fair."

"I'm not here to do fair, I'm here to solve cases," Kidd snapped. "And your behaviour directly impacts that, whether you believe it does or not."

Joe looked like he was maybe about to apologise, or at least about to do the decent thing and fuck off and leave Kidd alone. But apparently he thought better of it, hovering on the pavement outside the police station, trying to find a way to say whatever words were dancing on the tip of his tongue.

"What?" Kidd snapped.

"I know a lot about Kingston, Ben," Joe said, his voice low. "If you need my help—"

"I don't need your help," Kidd interrupted. "Based on your article, I'd say you're here sniffing around for more information about this case, and I'm here to tell you that I'm not going to give it to you."

"Because you don't have anything?"

"Because this investigation is ongoing," Kidd said. "Now if you actually have something that might help us with our investigation, then please, be my guest, go and talk to Diane and we will look into it, but if you don't, please piss off."

Joe looked like he may have had something else to say, that perhaps he was going to fight Kidd on this. But he thought better of it. Kidd was glad of that. He didn't want to argue with the lad, didn't want to get into a shouting match with someone who could smear him all over the internet if he wanted to. He'd done it before, what would stop him from doing it again?

Not a damn thing, Kidd thought.

Kidd waited for Joe to leave, watching him walk back towards town. He remembered what he'd come out here for, to get refreshments for his team. He headed into town, feeling like maybe he'd been too harsh with Joe as he picked up a selection of pastries and a full coffee order for his team. Normally, he would send someone else to do this, but he wanted to clear his head, wanted to get himself focussed, and sometimes a little walk was the way to do that.

He made it back to the station in good time, pleased to see that the journalists who had been practically camped out there before he'd left had now gone. So at least Diane would be off his back. But now DS Sanchez was waiting for him in reception. And that didn't feel like a good sign either.

"What's happened?" he asked, expecting the world to have imploded while he was in Pret.

"Nothing," she replied. "Someone is here to see you."

"Who?"

"Nina's ex-girlfriend."

CHAPTER
TWELVE

It took Kidd a moment to calibrate it in his head. He'd not been expecting that. No one had mentioned that Nina had a girlfriend, or an ex-girl-friend. Surely, that would be pertinent information someone should have given them. Why had no one mentioned it?

Kidd delivered the coffee and pastries to the Incident Room, filling in the rest of the team on where he and Zoe were going to be for the next little while. They were as surprised as he was that there was suddenly an ex-girlfriend in the picture. It was comforting to know that his confusion wasn't solitary.

Zoe had already brought her into the station, taking her through one of the smaller meeting rooms and sitting her down with a cup of tea, something to calm her nerves because Kidd had no doubt she was nervous.

When Kidd walked into the room, he was struck by how young she looked, how small, how frightened. She was wearing a pair of jeans and a baggy t-shirt, and Kidd could see her bag was a little way open, a green apron sticking out of the top of it, probably part of a work uniform. She'd been crying. Her eyes were puffy and red, her face a little blotchy. When she looked up at Kidd walking into the room with Zoe, it was a full deer-in-the-headlights moment. She was surprised to see him, surprised to see Zoe again. Maybe she'd lost track of where she was, of how long she'd been sitting there. She was on the verge of falling apart. But then, why wouldn't you be?

"Harper Gwynn?" Kidd said as he stepped into the room.

She nodded, putting her tea down and, getting to her feet, extending a hand to Kidd. He shook it. It wasn't what he'd expected from her; she seemed a little surprised by it herself. Maybe she thought that was the way you were supposed to greet a police officer. It was insanely polite.

"Thank you so much for coming in," Kidd said. "Please, take a seat."

"Thank you." Her voice was a little hoarse.

Kidd couldn't tell if she was a smoker, or if she

was just hoarse from crying. It could have been either.

"We would have contacted you sooner, but we... We didn't know you existed," Kidd said. "We have spoken to some of Nina's housemates, her family, we've even scoured her social media, and you weren't anywhere to be found."

Harper scoffed, picking her tea back up, cradling it in her hands like one would a baby bird, holding it close. "That's not too surprising."

"Why's that?" Kidd asked.

"We aren't together anymore," she said. "It wasn't the most amicable of breakups. She fully scrubbed me from her social media. It wouldn't surprise me if she didn't even tell her family about it. She wasn't in contact with them."

"And the housemates?"

"Oh, they didn't like me all that much," Harper replied. "I'm surprised that they didn't try and throw me under the bus for this, to be honest. It would suit them quite well for the psycho ex-girlfriend to be the murderer."

There was a definite chip on her shoulder. Something had happened with the housemates, that much was for sure. Kidd needed to get to the bottom of that, and to the bottom of why she and Nina had broken up. It could hold the key to something, at least.

"Tell me about your relationship with Nina," Kidd said.

"We have a pretty long history," she said. "Very on again, off again. You said they've not told you anything?"

"No one has even mentioned you."

"It's kind of insulting, actually," Harper said, a tinge of venom in every word. "We were together for almost two years. That's not an insignificant amount of time. You'd think I'd at least be a footnote, a thought." She swallowed. "You'd at least think I wouldn't have had to find out my ex-girlfriend is dead from some online rag that one of my colleagues saw."

"That's how you found out?"

"I was at work this morning—I work at The Coffee Bean in town, the little one on the corner near Bentalls," she said. "I... I got in, and one of my colleagues showed me an article they'd seen on their phone, dancing it around in front of my face like 'Isn't that your ex-girlfriend?' As if it was some big joke." She shook her head, took a sip of her tea. Her hands were shaking so badly, it was a wonder the drink was still in the cup at this point. "And I just... I looked at it and I read it and didn't want to believe it, but when I got on my lunch break, I looked at it properly and... it was her. Nina. My Nina." She paused, looking between the two detectives. "When I saw that same article had been updated with an appeal for information, I thought it was best that I come here and... tell you what I know."

The slight pause told Kidd that maybe Harper was the key they were looking for to truly unlock what had been going on with Nina, what her personal life had been like, where that money had come from. If Harper had been close to her, she might have insight that none of her housemates would have had.

"So you were together for two years?"

"It wasn't the most stable thing in the world," she said. "Maybe her housemates didn't think it was all that significant, but it was for me. I was devoted to her. She was just a bit... flighty."

"Flighty?"

"She didn't know what she wanted," Harper said. "One minute she wanted to settle down, then she wanted to be free and flit around and party and stuff. I'm not sure she knew what she wanted. And that's fine, not everyone does, but... I don't know. Just a bit of a mindfuck sometimes."

"Why did you break up?"

Harper snorted. "Which time?"

"The last time."

"It was hellfire," Harper said. "A proper screaming match about six months ago. We were at her house, her housemates were in their rooms, I think, and we were just fighting. I mean, we fought a lot. I can't even remember what it was about. Maybe she didn't want to be together anymore, maybe she had other stuff going on, and that was what was making her that way. She wasn't a very open person. She had a lot of shit going on. She didn't share it, and I'd... I'd push her."

"You'd push her?"

"I wanted her to talk to me," she said. "I wanted her to share things with me. I was her girlfriend, was it too much to ask to have a little bit of openness?"

"So you were fighting," Kidd said. He didn't want to weigh in on the particulars of their relationship. It wouldn't be helpful in her current state of mind, and it certainly wouldn't help them when it came to figuring out what had happened to Nina.

"And she told me she didn't want to see me again, never wanted to see me again, wanted me out of the house, sent me away with all of my stuff." She shook her head, her knee starting to bounce nervously. "We were in and out of each other's pockets. When it was on, it was on, when it was off, it was seriously off, but this was the first time she'd sent me away with my stuff. It felt like an ending, so I did what she asked."

"You stopped seeing her?"

"I avoided her if I could," Harper said. "She didn't come to The Coffee Bean anymore, and I made sure to avoid the clothes shop she worked at, the routes I knew she took from her house, I tried to make things easier, even if it hurt me to do it. I was actively avoiding her, which meant I was almost constantly thinking about her." She chuckled darkly. "You see where the mindfuck comes in, huh?"

"What was Nina like as a person?" Kidd said. "You said she had a lot of shit going on. What kind of shit are we talking about?"

"Well, there was the stuff with her parents," Harper said. "They weren't connected anymore because of her party lifestyle. They didn't want her to enjoy herself, I guess. She didn't like her job all that much. She was pretty directionless in that and felt like she needed a change, something to get her some more money."

"There's been an awful lot of talk about money problems," Kidd said. "How serious was it?"

Harper swallowed, looking between the two detectives. "This is what I wanted to come and talk to you about, really," she said. "Nina was in big trouble."

"How big?"

"She had maxed out all of her credit cards, she had personal loan debt, and then..." Another pause, another swallow, a wave of nervousness crashing over Harper before their very eyes. "Then there was the money that just showed up out of nowhere. Like all of her problems were solved, but they just seemed to get worse. She just got more stressed."

"Go back," Kidd said. "You said money appeared out of nowhere."

Harper was visibly nervous now. She'd put the teacup down and was picking at her fingers, unsure what to do with her hands now that she didn't have something to hold. There was a secret brewing, words waiting to form.

"Harper, please," Kidd said. "If Nina was in some kind of financial trouble and someone was helping to offset that, we need to know about it." He decided to take a punt. "Nina's purse was found at the club she was at last night with hundreds of pounds of cash in it. We don't know where it came from, we don't know who gave it to her, but someone walking around with a big wad of cash and winding up dead is rarely a good sign."

"She didn't tell me where it came from," Harper said. "She just said she was handling it and... and then the money showed up, and she kept spending. But it didn't solve the problem."

"How do you mean?"

"Because it gave her a cushion, it rescued her, and she thought it would continue to rescue her... until it didn't."

"Was Nina's life being threatened by whoever it was she was borrowing money from?"

"Yes," Harper said. "And she wouldn't let me help. And now she's dead. I don't... I don't know what to do."

And the truly scary thing in that moment was, neither did Kidd.

CHAPTER
THIRTEEN

I t put the fear of God into Kidd. It was all happening again. It was what had happened with Craig, it was what had happened with so many other people before, and here it was, right in front of his face.

They finished up with Harper, giving her some time to calm down, to get herself together. They suggested that she call someone to come and pick her up rather than go back to work, and Kidd left her with his number in case she needed someone to talk to about all of this.

The death of Nina had rattled her, and the fact that she had been sitting on that information was clearly enough to make her feel guilty about it. She still cared about Nina, that much was obvious, and to have this happen to her, to know that Nina had been in trouble and she hadn't been able to help her, had Harper falling apart.

"What do you think of Harper, then?" Zoe asked when she'd left, the two of them heading to the little kitchen so they could speak privately. They sat down at the little table in there rather than heading back to the Incident Room. Kidd needed some time to process everything.

"I think she's keeping something from us," Kidd said.

Zoe blinked. "What?"

"The name of that person who was lending Nina money is so bloody important," Kidd said. "How can she not know who that was?"

"Well, she did say that Nina was quite closed off, that she didn't share much," Zoe said. "Maybe that was just another thing she didn't share."

"Maybe," Kidd replied, but he didn't want to believe it. He wanted to believe that Harper knew because then there would be a connection some-where to be made, a lead that they could follow instead of a dead end. That bouncy feeling he'd had earlier, that feeling that progress was being made, had quickly faded into a distant memory.

"Do you think she's involved?"

Kidd considered it for a moment. She had come to them rather than them having to track her down. She hadn't even been mentioned by any of their interviewees. She was trying to help as best she could, trying to make sure the case was solved. So maybe not.

"No," Kidd said. "I think she's hurting and genuinely trying to help. She's hiding just how much she's hurting because... I don't know why."

"I think she probably feels embarrassed about being sad," Zoe said. "She wasn't with Nina anymore; she wasn't her person, so to be mourning her intensely might feel a little embarrassing. Like people are judging her. She strikes me as the kind of person who doesn't like to be judged like that. I kind of get it."

Zoe went quiet, and Kidd realised that they weren't talking about Harper anymore. He'd not been there for her after Owen had died, and he knew that. He had up and left because he was having his own feelings, his own problems. They'd not had the time to talk about exactly how things had been for her during that time.

"And how are you doing with all of that?" he asked.

Zoe blinked, looking up at him. "What's that now?"

"We're not talking about Harper and Nina," Kidd said. "I think we're talking about Zoe and Owen. I know we didn't have a lot of time to talk about it, and I've been somewhat hesitant to bring it up since I've been back because..."

"Go on."

"Because you seem so happy with Seth, for one," Kidd said. "And the last thing I want to do is dredge up some kind of history that's going to cause you pain. That would be really shitty of me, I think."

"It wouldn't be," she replied. "You're right, we didn't get a chance to talk about it because... You had your own stuff to deal with. I didn't realise quite how much stuff because you did a fantastic job of keeping all of the Andrea and Craig stuff from me until I absolutely needed to know about it."

"Yeah, I'm sorry about all that, in case I haven't apologised already," Kidd said. "Everything that happened with that, plus John, plus Craig, plus Owen, it was a lot. Running might not have seemed like the right option, but I had to do it. I needed to get away."

"I'm just glad you finally told me about it," she said. "I think if you hadn't, that would have been the end of our friendship."

"Well then, I'm glad I did," he said with a chuckle. "So, how are things in that department?" he asked again. "I want you to know that if you want to talk about it, I'm here for you."

Zoe took a moment, having a sip of her coffee, wincing at how hot it still was, before placing it down on the table in front of her. She wrapped her hands around the cup and let out a heavy breath.

"I'm okay," she said. "I still think about him from time to time because... well... I still work in the same building. So much of my life hasn't changed, even though he's no longer in it. But also so much has. Things have moved on, which they are bound to do. Basically, I'm okay. But I knew that you coming back would be hard."

"How do you mean?"

"You come back and you bring all this history with you," Zoe replied. "I'm not trying to get at you here, I promise, but you have so much history here; we have so much history together. You coming back brings back a lot of memories and thoughts. I'm okay, but I reserve the right to not be okay at some undisclosed point in the future."

Kidd chuckled. "I think that's entirely fair," he replied. "So, the case?"

"The case," she said, happy to draw a line under that particular conversation. "I think she's telling us as much as she can, and our next port of call needs to be getting that CCTV from The Snake Pit and finding out exactly what went on there. There's something we're missing; I can just feel it."

"I spoke to Joe Warrington earlier on," Kidd said.

Zoe hit him on the arm. "Why didn't you bloody mention that?"

"Because it's hardly a news story," Kidd replied. "He's a journalist, and he is the one who leaked that bloody name, so he was outside when those other journalists were. I think he's trying to make it seem like he has more information than he actually does."

"There's a surprise."

"I tore into him a bit."

"Well, you've not spoken to him since what happened with Owen," Zoe said. "He doesn't know what you've been through, apart from knowing that you'd taken a leave of absence." She paused. "He might not be lying, you know. He might... he might have information that could be useful."

Kidd shook his head. "It's not a door I necessarily want to open, but one that I may have to. He seems to have all the gossip in town, who knows what he might know."

Zoe sucked in a breath. "I... I may have done that. And it didn't end well."

"How so?"

"I spoke to him about a case while you were away, the one that helped us catch DI McMichaels out," Zoe said. "He gave me some information, I gave him some back. And then he expected that same level of treatment on the next case and... and I didn't give it to him."

"What happened there?"

"He wasn't thrilled about it, let's just say," Zoe said. "He felt like I owed him something. Give him one little nugget of information, and suddenly he feels like he's part of the force."

"So no love lost there."

"Oh, he'll never speak to me again," she said.

"Both a blessing and a curse for sure, but he's pissed at me."

Kidd considered this. A lot really had happened since he'd been away. The last thing he wanted to do was get on the wrong side of Joe Warrington.

"Maybe that's a last resort kind of door, then," Kidd said. "We'll keep him at arm's length for now."

Zoe seemed to relax a little at that. "Sounds like a plan."

CHAPTER
FOURTEEN

Back in the Incident Room, they filled in the rest of the team on their interview with Harper. It hadn't presented them with any more leads, but it had certainly filled in some of the gaps in Nina's life. She was a party girl, she was having money troubles, and maybe if they managed to get to the bottom of where that money was coming from, maybe, just maybe, they'd be able to trace it back to whoever had killed Nina.

Powell got a photo of Harper from social media and put it on the board with the others. She was a connection they had if they needed any more information, and Kidd was still certain she was holding out on them.

Kidd desperately didn't want it to be connected to Andrea. Her grip on the town already felt vice-like, another death on her hands, more spilled blood. Kidd didn't want to think about it.

He made a call to Perkins in Kingston Town Centre. It was a small clothes shop on the Old London Road. Kidd walked past it on his way to and from work, and now it would always be connected to Nina. It was just another ghost to add to the ever-growing list.

Blake Grover hadn't come into work that day. He was supposed to, but he hadn't shown up.

"You think he's hiding?" Zoe asked.

"I'm hoping he's just hungover," Kidd said. "But if he's not in tomorrow, we're going to have to play a little game of hide and seek with Blake."

JOHN

Don't forget, dinner at your sister's tonight. Please tell me you're coming.

KIDD

I'm just leaving work. I'll come home and get changed and we'll head on over.

HE DID EXACTLY THAT, DISMISSING THE TEAM AND heading home, where he got ready in record time to leave the house with John, the two of them setting off on foot to Liz's house.

"And how was it to be properly back at work?" John asked, as they made their way over, the two of them walking hand in hand through the back streets of Kingston.

"Straight in at the deep end," Kidd replied. "I don't think there could have been a more serious case for me to come back to if we tried."

"And you're loving every second of it?" John said.

"Yes," Kidd admitted. "I actually am. There's a bit of meat to it. You know me, John, I need it."

"You should be studied," he said. "I, on the other hand, am back in the office, and things have pretty much gone entirely back to normal."

"You're joking," Kidd said. "After everything that happened down in Southend, they're just acting like nothing's happened? Like it's all the same?"

"There was a brief chat about it," John said. "They don't want us talking to the press, they don't want us having any opinions on Michael Smithson or his antics." He shook his head. "The books are staying on sale, though."

"They're not!"

John snorted. "There's money to be made, Ben," he said. "And where there's money to be made, my boss is all over it!"

"Christ, she sounds like a nightmare."

"She is," John said flatly. "So I've got her breathing down my neck, my authors are absolutely feral because it's the new year and they're either freaking out about new releases or trying to get new books over the line so that they can get new contracts." He shook his head. "It's like I've not even been away."

"So what you're saying is that you need a nice relaxing dinner with good company and wine tonight to get you through it?" Kidd suggested, somewhat hopefully. He didn't necessarily want to be dragging John to his sister's house if he wasn't in the mood.

John smiled. "That's exactly what I'm saying."

The house was a hive of activity. Tilly and Tim were both excited to see their uncle, and even John, this time around, who had become something of a staple at these dinners. They were coming around to him, especially as he had plied them with free books that he'd managed to pilfer from his publisher.

"Well, well, well," Liz said. "I was half expecting you to cancel on me."

"I rarely cancel on you," Kidd said, pulling her into a hug. He tried not to, but every now and again, work would get in the way and it had to take priority. Though he was going to be better at that. It was one of his resolutions for the year, to stop letting work get so in the way of everything. He already expected it to go poorly.

"I know, I know. We're just glad you're here."

"Greg's in?" Kidd said. "I thought he'd be working late."

"Managed to swing the night off," Liz replied. "So we're a full house tonight. A slightly less full house once these munchkins go to bed." She said it loud enough for Greg to hear in the other room, and Kidd heard the TV switch off just before Greg appeared in the doorway.

He greeted the pair of them, taking his cue to run the kids upstairs and start getting them ready for bed. Kidd had seen them a fair amount over Christmas, so it wasn't the end of the world that he wasn't seeing much of the children tonight, but it was still a shame they'd arrived as late as they had.

How is that resolution going? he thought.

Once the children had been put to bed, Liz dished up dinner and opened a nice bottle of wine, pouring everyone large glasses before she took a seat and encouraged everyone to tuck into the spread she had spent a lot of the afternoon and evening making.

"This is a bloody Christmas dinner," Kidd said. "It looks incredible."

"Glad you added that last part," Liz said. "It started as me just wanting to get rid of some leftover veg and potatoes, but then I thought, why not just do the whole thing and treat ourselves? The start of the year is so bleak, might as well have some nice food. Go on, please, help yourselves."

They filled their plates, Kidd deciding to embrace the late Christmas dinner, and after the day he'd had, he felt like he deserved it.

"So, you're back at work?" Greg asked. "I know you didn't spend a lot of time relaxing while you were away—Liz kept me filled in on your adventures down on the coast—but it must be strange to be back in Kingston."

"It is," Kidd replied. "Everything has changed, but at the same time so much has stayed the same. New team member started while I was away, so that's an adjustment, and a new case was dumped on my desk this morning, so it's all go go go."

"No time to sit down and dwell on being back," Greg suggested.

"Well, I had to get through a fitness test and occupational health evaluations first," Kidd replied. "So actually, that was my rest time, if you can believe it."

"You got through the fitness test, then?" Liz said.

"Alright, Liz," Kidd replied.

"What?"

"That sounded like a snipe."

"I wasn't sniping!" she said, her cheeks tingeing pink. "You just always say how hard they are. That was me trying to ask if it was difficult. I wasn't suggesting you couldn't do it."

"He almost couldn't," John chimed in. "Didn't you nearly pass out?"

"I did," Kidd said sheepishly.

"And you had to lie down and then they brought you a Mars bar for the sugar rush."

"Oh my God, spill all my secrets, why don't you?"

Kidd said with a laugh. "All true. It was horrible, and I need to get back to running so that next time I do it, I maybe don't need to have an emergency Mars bar."

"I've found that it always helps to have an emergency Mars bar lying around," Liz said. "You never know when you're going to need that extra boost."

"Then why not have a Boost?" Greg suggested.

"Touché," Liz replied.

They continued to talk about how work was going for each of them, and how, while Kidd and John's lives had changed so dramatically over the past six months, Greg and Liz's life had pretty much stayed entirely the same. They'd had a relationship blip in the middle of last year, but now were finding it to be stronger than ever before.

"Tilly will be starting school in September," Liz said. "And that's a terrifying thought. I don't know what I'm going to do with myself."

"So it's just going to be you and Tim all day?" Kidd asked.

"Well, I'm thinking of going back to work," Liz said. "It's been such a long time since I've done it, and I used to love working so... I think Tim will end up in nursery, and I'll end up back in the workforce in some way. Things will be changing for us this time around. It's frightening."

"As someone who has had a year of great change," Kidd started. "I can tell you that it's not so bad. It can be scary at times, but you just have to get yourself through it. You'll have an absolute ball going back to work. Do you know what you're going to do?"

Liz was practically giddy with it. "No, not a clue," she replied. "The world is my oyster, which is both exciting and entirely paralysing. I could do absolutely anything, which means my brain doesn't really know where to put me."

"You'll figure it out," Kidd said. "And if you need anything from me, just give me a shout."

"You offering yourself up for the school run?" Liz said.

Kidd hadn't considered that. "It sounds like it would be a bit out of my comfort zone, but if you need me to pick up Tilly or take her to school, I can do that. Or at least try."

"That's all I ask," Liz replied.

Their evening continued on, the conversation descending in and out of talking about work and family and New Year's resolutions and beyond. It was the kind of dinner that Kidd had missed while he'd been away, that connection with his family that had been so key to his life in Kingston. It was nice to have that back. Not that he would tell Liz. She would probably just make a vomiting noise and make fun of him if he dared try.

CHAPTER
FIFTEEN

K idd and John said their goodbyes to Liz and Greg at around ten pm, all of them feeling more than a little bit worn down by their return to normal life post-Christmas and New Year. That and the fact that they all had early starts in the morning.

"I hate that we are the kinds of people who have early starts," Liz said.

"That's practically everyone," Kidd replied.

"I know, but when it was Mum and Dad talking about it, I never thought it would be us," she said. "I just imagined more of a life of leisure rather than one of... well... whatever I have."

She gave him a hug, squeezing him tight. "Make sure you take care of yourself," she said. "And if you dare disappear on me like that again—"

"I know, I know, death on swift wings."

"Something like that," she said. "Don't be a stranger. The kids miss you. I miss you."

"I'll message you," Kidd replied, heading down the garden path with John and starting their journey home.

It wasn't too far, but John took them in a different direction, walking them around town, almost guiding them away from the house a little way, walking through a very quiet Kingston, past the people heading for their nights out, the two of them just chattering away.

But then the conversation died off, and silence crept in, and Kidd's head started to get loud, very loud indeed. He lived so close to Liz. It was a shame he didn't see her more.

"What are you thinking about?" John asked.

"How I'm a terrible brother, mostly," Kidd replied. "Making promises to myself that I'm going to be better because my sister lives a stone's throw away, and I feel like I never see her."

"You know that's not true," John replied, taking Kidd's hand and giving it a squeeze. "You've been away for the last few months. How were you meant to see her when you were trying to get your head back together?"

"Well, that's true," Kidd replied. "I just feel bad. I have a niece who's about to go to school, everything is changing and moving on, and I don't want to miss too much, you know?"

"I know," John replied. "But you're doing fine. And look, I imagine this is coming from a place of guilt about you up and leaving before, back when things got bad with Craig vanishing. But this is different. You needed the break. We both did."

Kidd was incredibly grateful for John in that moment. They'd been through a lot together, not all of it good, and to have come through the other side and still be together, stronger than ever, felt like an overwhelming positive in Kidd's life. He didn't want to fuck that up.

They carried on, circling past The Druids Head, heading towards the big John Lewis to loop back on themselves through town and back to Kidd's house. It was nice to be out in the evening, to be walking around, to be unwinding at the end of their day. After the snap back to reality that Kidd had that morning, he needed it. But as they got to the big John Lewis, Kidd couldn't help but turn his head towards the riverside.

"What are you looking at?" John asked.

Kidd swallowed. "Found a body by the river this morning," Kidd said. "She'd been in the club last night, The Snake Pit."

"And it's open tonight?"

"Certainly looks like it." There were people queuing up outside, snaking down from the entrance and towards the John Lewis. "Cordon must have been cleared," Kidd said. "People just moved on without... Without thinking about it, I suppose. That's a bit sad, isn't it?"

"Just a touch," John said, trying to pull Kidd in the opposite direction. "Ben—"

Kidd pulled him in the other direction, walking towards where the revellers were queuing up, waiting to go inside. Boys in t-shirts and vests, girls in short skirts and mini dresses, all of them stumbling around a bit, all of them in far too few layers for how absolutely bloody freezing it was.

"You're not trying to pull me in there for a drink, are you?" John said. "Because I don't think it's our scene. We are at least ten years older than all of these people."

"Conservative estimate."

"I'm trying to shield my ego."

"You don't look more than nine years older," Kidd said.

John laughed. "Nice, lovely, thanks for that," John replied. "Come on, you're acting weird, what are you doing?"

Kidd wanted to go in there, he wanted to talk to people, talk to the manager, talk to Seth, get the CCTV, keep everything moving on this case because this place being open, people still coming out to party when Nina Hawkins died less than twenty-four hours ago didn't sit right with him. It made him feel like people were forgetting, and he didn't want people to forget.

"Let's go," John said. "You've had a drink, you're not thinking clearly. Come back to it tomorrow, when you're on the clock."

Kidd hesitated. He wanted to know more, he wanted to keep looking into it, but he also knew in his heart of hearts that John was right. He was in no fit state to start questioning people tonight. He needed to get some rest, and then he would get back to it.

He was about to turn back to the high street when he saw a figure standing by Kingston Bridge. They looked at him, looked him dead in the face. They were staring him down. And Kidd recognised them.

He knew that face, even though they had a hood up, a nearby streetlamp illuminated what was hidden there.

That can't be... Kidd thought, as the person turned away and crossed the road.

Craig Peyton.

Craig Peyton was back.

CHAPTER
SIXTEEN

Harper Gwynn was beyond desperate to switch off right now. She'd not taken the advice of the two kind detectives who had listened to her blubbering away at the station earlier that day. She'd gone back to work, she'd tried to continue her shift, tried to ignore the members of staff staring at her, the members of staff whispering behind her back.

A couple of them took the time to make sure she was okay, to make sure that she wasn't about to fall apart. She was. But she wasn't about to let them know that.

On her way home, she debated calling Nina's housemates, the girls who hadn't been keen on being her friend, the ones who would also be grieving right now. There was a chance that they could build something out of this, wasn't there? There was a chance that maybe they wouldn't all remain disconnected while their collective worlds fell apart.

But they already had each other. Harper was the one who was all alone.

She picked up some food on the way home, a bottle of wine to ease the aching in her heart, and headed back to her flat. She was glad that she'd tidied the place before work, that she'd taken the time to make things clean, to make things tidy. It felt like she was coming home to somewhere a little more comfortable. A little less... lonely.

She turned on the lights. It was a studio apartment she'd moved into a couple of years ago. Nina had been there on more than one occasion, she'd spent time there, she'd spent a lot of time there. They had looked at proper one-bedroom flats together there, places they could live together, and then it had all fallen apart. And now she truly was alone without her. How quickly times had changed.

She turned on the lamps dotted around the room, switching off the big light because the glare was just too much tonight. She needed the place to feel cosy.

She put her shopping down on the kitchen counter and suddenly stopped. Something felt off. There were eyes on her. She could feel it, like something tickling at the back of her head, the smallest little inkling.

She turned sharply and saw her open door, the empty space in the frame, and she let out a breath.

"Idiot," she breathed. She'd left the door open. She'd been in such a hurry to get inside, such a rush to get on with her evening, that she'd left the door open. She shook her head and walked over, pulling the door closed.

And then she felt a pain in the back of her head, something hard striking her. She stumbled, almost hitting the floor, barely able to keep herself upright.

Hands closed around her throat before she had a chance to do anything about it, before she could stop them. She tried to pull away, but her energy was sapped, barely there.

She clawed at the hands. There was a scream as they let go, as Harper stumbled, trying desperately to pull the air into her lungs. She clattered into the coffee table, she tripped. She hit the floor this time, and it was enough time for her assailant to reach her, rolling her onto her back, straddling her, stopping her from raising her arms.

And in that moment, Harper got a good look at her attacker, at the person who was so desperate to kill her, the same way they had likely killed Nina.

She stared up into the face of someone she recognised, as the hands closed around her neck once again, as the breath was pushing from her lungs, as the darkness finally closed in.

CHAPTER
SEVENTEEN

K idd barely slept that night. He went through the motions of getting himself ready for bed, washing his face, brushing his teeth, winding down a little bit by pretending to read a book, but his brain could not focus on anything else except for the face of Craig Peyton, staring daggers at him from down the road.

In fairness, Kidd had been tipsy. It was very possible that he'd been imagining things, that the person had just looked similar to Craig rather than actually being Craig. But he was so sure. He knew that face so well.

Why would Craig have come back again? After everything that happened with Andrea the last time, after the danger he'd put himself in, why would he come back?

Kidd went through all of the possible reasons in his head. Had he decided to come back after Kidd told him about what happened with Andrea? Could it have been something to do with Billy back in Southend? There were so many questions that Kidd suddenly had that he found himself reaching for his phone in the middle of the night and scrolling to the last phone number he had for Craig Peyton.

He debated calling it, he debated sending a message, he debated blocking it and removing that temptation from his life entirely because he could do without the hassle.

Whenever Craig showed up, trouble often followed. Kidd didn't want any more trouble. He wanted his personal life to be quiet. But here Craig was, showing up again, ready to wreak havoc.

He had no proof of that, of course. He could have been imagining it, after all. But what if?

And that was the train of thought that Kidd was aboard for the entire night, a circular track stopping at the same old stations over and over and over again until his alarm clock went off and there was no further chance to sleep.

So much for him getting a decent night's sleep ahead of what would definitely be a busy day.

He got himself up, showered, pulled on a fresh suit to try and make himself feel some semblance of alive, and got himself ready to go. He made his way downstairs to see John standing in the kitchen, dressing gown on, making himself a cup of tea.

"Bloody hell, you're off early," John said. "You okay?"

"Yeah," Kidd replied. "Couldn't sleep. Figured I'd get a jump on the day."

"Yeah, I noticed you were tossing and turning a bit," John replied. "Everything okay?"

Kidd hesitated. He didn't know if it was even worth mentioning to John. He didn't want to rock the boat, nor did he want to make John worry about something that he may well have imagined. It might end up being a massive waste of energy. That was the last thing he wanted to do.

"Yeah, fine," Kidd said. "Just a lot on my mind. I didn't keep you up, did I?"

"Oh, God, no," John said. "One glass of wine, and I was totally knocked out. How I'm going to survive when the industry parties start up is beyond me. I might have to pace myself."

"Heaven forbid," Kidd replied. "I'll see you later, yeah? Didn't mean to disturb you."

They said their goodbyes, and Kidd made his way back out into the world. The coolness of the day hit him square in the face, lifting him a touch, forcing him to wake up. It was bracing.

He walked out of his house, making his way down the street and toward The Snake Pit. The street was a bit of a mess after last night, plastic cups littering the pavement, bins overflowing with them. Why people had taken their drinks outside was beyond Kidd. It had been freezing last night.

He stopped as he reached the point where he'd seen Craig standing the night before. He looked at The Snake Pit, across the river, at the cars passing over Kingston Bridge. He didn't know what he was expecting by standing there. That Craig would just appear again? That he would just show up and explain why he was back? If he was back?

Kidd shook his head. He was losing his mind here. Maybe it was the stress of being back in Kingston, or back at work. Or maybe it was because Craig had come up on one of his last cases in Southend. He'd even called him for Zoe, and his friend, Billy, had been part of something pretty major there. Could he be back for that? Was Billy going to be the next person he saw standing on a corner, waiting for him?

Kidd turned to head down the stairs and onto the riverside, but noticed that the doors to The Snake Pit were propped open with a bin. He could wait until later. He could come back here with another member of his team, do it when he was officially on the clock, but this opportunity was right in front of him. It felt worth getting a jump on it.

As far as he knew, Seth was working as hard as he could to get them the CCTV they needed from the outside of the building, but if Lawrence said he was going to be here all day, surely it would be him who'd left the door propped open. It was practically an invitation. Kidd was treating it as one, at least.

"Hello?" Kidd called when he stepped inside. The space was somehow worse than he remembered it from just the day prior. Whoever had been here last night had torn the place apart. There were plastic cups everywhere, little shot glasses dotted all over the floor, and a vague, sickly-sweet smell that turned Kidd's stomach.

"We don't open until tonight, please fuck off while I'm airing the stench of Uni students out of here!" The voice was a little hoarse, coming from somewhere behind the bar. Kidd couldn't see exactly where. He at least knew that it wasn't Seth.

"Lawrence Brewer?" Kidd called out.

A man stepped out from a darkened corner. He was tall, broad, and his bald head was shiny in the fluorescent day-lights of the club. He did not look pleased to see Kidd, not one little bit.

"Who wants to know?"

"Detective Inspector Benjamin Kidd, we spoke on the phone yesterday."

"Bloody hell," Lawrence said, checking his phone. "Early start for you, eh?"

"I could say the same," Kidd replied. "What are you doing here so early?"

"Short-staffed last night, none of the cleaning got done, so yours truly has to do it," he grumbled.

"We've got to open tonight, and I don't want to leave it for my staff tonight, to clean up yesterday's mess."

"How enterprising."

"Oh yes, that's what I do it for, not so I don't piss off the few staff I have," he replied. "Any chance we can do this later?"

"No," Kidd replied.

"I've got a lot to do and—"

"I wasn't planning on doing this now, Mr Brewer. I was going to give you a call and pop down later, but I saw the lights were on and figured I would take the opportunity when it presented itself."

"Now who's being enterprising?"

"No matter what it is that you have to do, Mr Brewer, I should think that talking about this case trumps all of that."

Kidd could see him hesitating, potentially trying to find a way to get out of having this conversation. But Kidd was standing firm, not moving from his position a little way away from the bar. He wasn't about to turn away. He wanted to talk to Lawrence Brewer, and it was going to happen right now.

"You know why I'm here, Mr Brewer, there's no need for us to dance around it," Kidd said. "I need the CCTV from the night before last in your club. I know one of your staff members has been trying to get it for me, but I've come right to the source. We need it sooner than soon."

"We're doing our best—"

"Your best isn't good enough," Kidd said. "And I want to talk to you about what's happened in your club."

"I don't feel like there's anything to talk about," Lawrence said. Kidd could hardly believe what he was hearing. "What's happened has happened. It's now your job to get it solved, to find out what happened. I don't need you poking around, asking me questions about it."

"Mr Brewer—"

"I can get the CCTV to you. Always happy to cooperate with your lot on stuff. We've got nothing to hide here."

"You're acting like you do," Kidd said. "Or at the very least, that you don't care that a dead body has been found outside your club."

"You say outside my club, I'd say down by the river," Lawrence said with a smirk. "She might have been in my club before it happened, but she didn't die here, Detective, you're not about to get us shut down, you have no grounds."

Kidd knew he was right, but Lawrence was starting to piss him off. If he had the grounds to shut the place down, he would have done it already. He needed that CCTV, and he needed it yesterday.

"I'm not trying to ruffle any feathers here, Detective, but you've come in here and started throwing your weight around and, frankly, it's not warranted," Lawrence said. "You're in the middle of an investigation. I appreciate that it's a very stressful time for you, but you are barking up the wrong tree if you think you can come in here and start shouting the odds at me."

"Get me the CCTV," Kidd said. "I want it by the end of today, or I'll be coming back here."

CHAPTER
EIGHTEEN

I t wasn't the kind of conversation that Kidd was hoping to have with Lawrence. He'd hoped for it to be more productive, more civil, but he seemed determined to make sure that it wasn't going to be anything of the sort.

Kidd made his way to the station, heading into the Incident Room and managing to get there before the rest of his team. He spent some time responding to emails, seeing that there were new articles popping up about Nina Hawkins, a few that were digging into her past, talking about the promising young woman who had been found dead by Kingston Riverside. They didn't know the cause of death, of course, but they were whipping the general public up into a frenzy, nevertheless.

Kidd couldn't stand the press.

He leant back in his chair, his gaze finding the

ceiling, and his mind wandering once again to Craig Peyton. How likely was it that seeing him was a figment of his imagination? How likely was it that he had come back to stir up trouble for him once again? He didn't want to think about it, he wanted to be able to move on with his life, but no matter what he did, Craig always seemed to reappear. Kidd wondered if the only way out for them would be together. If they were doomed to do this dance until one of them—

His phone rang on his desk. It was a pleasing break from the runaway freight train in his mind.

He picked up the phone.

"Am I speaking to Detective Inspector Benjamin Kidd?"

"Yes," Kidd replied. "Who is this?"

"Helene Daniel," the voice replied. There was a slight accent to it, something European, perhaps. Kidd couldn't quite place it. "I'm working on your autopsy report, is now a good time?"

"As good a time as any," Kidd said. "Thank you for working on it so quickly, What have you got for me?"

"Well, your team wasn't too keen on letting me do it at my own pace," Helene replied. Kidd could hear the smirk as she spoke. "I got it done as quickly as I could, figured time must have been of the essence if DC Powell was blowing up my phone every couple of hours."

"Thank you."

"The death was caused by strangulation," she started. "I think you knew that much, the marks around the neck are prominent."

"Any prints?"

"Gloves," Helene replied. "Whoever your killer is, they knew what they were doing. They weren't about to get caught out by something like that."

"So it was premeditated," Kidd replied. He'd figured as much, this just about confirmed it.

"There were drugs in her system, too," Helene continued. "Flunitrazepam was found."

"She'd been spiked?" Kidd sat up a little straighter. He knew that was Rohypnol, a common drug used to spike drinks.

"It would appear that way," Helene replied. "I'll be able to get a full report over to you this afternoon, but these are the top-line notes. Figured it was important to get those to you quicker than anything else."

"Thank you, Helene. I appreciate that." Kidd hung up the phone. He needed that CCTV, he needed them to act quicker. He may even need to get The Snake Pit closed for a short time.

So much for not being able to shut them down, Kidd thought. They needed to eliminate The Snake Pit from the conversation. With the date-rape drug circulating, surely it could be a dangerous place for anyone to be right now. He couldn't just leave it open.

He was about to pick up the phone to see if

Weaver was in yet, when his mobile rang on his desk, the DCI's name in big white letters across the screen.

"Boss?" Kidd said as he answered. "Are you psychic? I was just thinking about you."

"Well, I'm flattered," Weaver replied. "You at the station yet?"

"Yeah, boss, already here," Kidd said. "Got the autopsy report through for Nina Hawkins."

"Hold that thought," Weaver replied. "I've found something you might want to take a look at."

Kidd's blood ran cold. "What's happened?"

"Remember the girl who came and spoke to you yesterday?"

"Harper Gwynn?" Kidd replied. "What's happened? Is she okay?"

"Very much not okay, Kidd," Weaver replied. "Harper is dead."

CHAPTER
NINETEEN

Kidd called Sanchez on his way to the crime scene, dropping messages off to the rest of the team to let them know where he was going to be and to carry on with the search for information about Nina. It was only as he sent those messages that he realised they wouldn't know about the Rohypnol. Everything was moving so quickly, he could feel the entire case running away from him if he didn't grab hold of it tightly with both hands.

Harper lived in an apartment block just a little way outside of Kingston, up on Villiers Avenue, most of the way to Surbiton. He remembered the address from a previous case, when someone had been killed in a building not too far from this one by Tony Warrington. This area was starting to get a reputation.

The police were already in attendance, the entire

place cordoned off, the residents outside in the freezing-cold morning air. They didn't look too happy, standing around in dressing gowns and wrapped in blankets that they'd managed to grab on their way out the door.

There were uniformed officers talking to some of them, trying to get information, get statements from people, see if they'd heard anyone coming in last night, if they saw anything that might help them.

Weaver was at the door to the block, holding the door open, waiting for Kidd.

"That was as quick as you could make it?" Weaver said with a smirk, shaking his wrist, showing off his watch. "You stop to get coffee or something?"

"Thought it might be pertinent to let the team know where I'd got to," Kidd said. "They're going to keep on the Nina stuff; Sanchez is meeting us here."

"Sanchez is already here." Zoe's voice came from behind him. She was a little out of breath, like she'd maybe jogged most of the way here. "Harper Gwynn?"

"Yep," Kidd said, turning his attention back to Weaver. "What are we dealing with here?"

"It's... It's pretty bad," Weaver said, nodding to them both to join him inside. They started along the corridor and up the stairs, Weaver talking to them every step of the way. "I got the call this morning from uniforms. One of them had greeted her when she'd come in yesterday, knew she had something to do with you because Sanchez had been the one to pick her up," he continued. "I called you, and now here we are."

"What happened?" Kidd asked.

"Whoever did this knew exactly what they were doing," Weaver said. "It was targeted, and from what I can tell, they'd hardly left a bloody trace anywhere."

"Forensics already here?"

"They're on their way," Weaver said. "Shoe covers on. Don't bloody touch anything."

When they got to the third floor, they did as they were told, shoe covers were put on, blue plastic gloves pulled on over sweaty palms as they made their way to the door. The two officers standing outside offered the detectives a nod as they stepped aside to let them pass.

It was an open-plan studio apartment. The bed to one side, a kitchen/dining room to the other. There was a small sofa, a coffee table, and a little TV. It was a tight space, but maybe it was all that Harper could afford. Maybe it was all the space she needed. She didn't seem to have a lot of stuff, and anything that she did have was currently scattered across the floor, surrounding her prone body.

There was no blood. There was no drama or grotesqueness to how the body had been left. She was lying there as if asleep, as if she had just decided that it would be more comfortable to sleep there than it would be to sleep on the bed.

Were her eyes not vacant, her head lolled to one side, dark red handprints around her neck, it might have been easy to keep pretending that she was just asleep.

"When was she found?" Kidd asked.

"There was a dad taking his children to school this morning," Weaver said gravely. "He noticed that the door was wide open, sent the little ones downstairs to wait for him while he came in to check. He saw her on the floor, saw her eyes staring, and rang us." He took a breath. "What did she tell you yesterday?"

"Not a whole lot," Kidd replied. "We didn't even know she existed until she showed up on our doorstep. No one was paying her any attention whatsoever."

"She didn't come up at all?"

"Not with the housemates, not with the parents," Kidd clarified. "I thought it was strange too, if she'd not seen the article online, she wouldn't even have known that Nina was dead."

And she wouldn't be dead now, Kidd thought. Whoever had done this obviously thought she had given away a lot more information than she had. They were trying to shut her up, and they'd succeeded. What else had she known? Had Kidd

142

been right all along? Had there been pieces missing from the information she'd given them yesterday?

Kidd looked around. The place looked like it had been torn apart. If nothing else, it looked like Harper put up a pretty decent fight. But it had come to nothing in the end.

"We might be able to find something amongst all this," Weaver said. "Place looks like a bloody bomb has hit it."

"Well, hopefully it gives us a heading," Kidd replied.

Weaver's phone chirped in his pocket, and he took it out. "Forensics are here," he said. "Best we get out of their way." He made his way out of the apartment, Kidd sticking around, looking at everything, like some kind of clue was going to jump out at him. Nothing did. He would have to wait. He would have to keep looking.

He looked down at Harper's body once again. If his hunch was right, that she was hiding something, and if his other hunch that Andrea was involved in all of this was right, then he knew that she was capable of something like this, he knew what she could do given half a chance if she felt like somebody had crossed her. The thought made Kidd's blood run cold.

DS Sanchez took hold of Kidd's arm, pulling him to the door, taking him back outside. "What are you thinking?"

"What do you mean?"

"I can see your brain going at a million miles a minute. Are you okay? What are you thinking?"

Kidd hesitated. He'd not mentioned the reappearance of Craig, but it suddenly seemed suspicious that he'd shown up just at the moment when another person in this case turned up dead, just at the point when he was starting to think that his sister, Andrea, was the one behind it all.

"I'm thinking of Andrea," Kidd said, trying to keep his voice steady.

"You really—?"

"People who cross her seem to end up in a pretty sorry state," Kidd interrupted. "If Harper was coming to us with information and she was caught out by someone close to Andrea, or seen walking out of the station, then that could have put a target on her back."

"But she didn't tell us anything," Zoe said. "Not really. She told us about Nina being short of money, and that she was borrowing from somewhere, but she didn't tell us where. She told us she didn't know."

"And the fact that she's dead makes me think that my hunch was right," Kidd said. "She knew more than she was letting on, and that's why she's..." He looked back at the apartment building. There was CCTV on the door, there would likely be something in the corridors. There would be something here that would help them track down whoever was responsible.

He was in trouble here, and he knew it. They needed to act fast.

"We need to get back to the station," Kidd said. "The rest of the team will have shown up by now. We need to keep moving on this."

"What do we do next?" Zoe asked.

Kidd swallowed. "I'm not sure," he said. "I need to figure it out, though."

CHAPTER
TWENTY

Kidd waited with the forensics team, getting as much information from them as he could before he made his way back to the station. He stepped into the Incident Room, wasting no time in filling everyone in on what he and Zoe had seen that morning.

"We need to start looking into Harper's life, too," Kidd said. "We've got ID, let's find a next of kin and make sure they know what's happened, and let's find out who else she was hanging out with. Not just Nina."

"She gave us information yesterday," Janya said. "Do you think—?"

"Yes," Kidd interrupted. "I think whoever did this was trying to stop us digging deeper into what she told us. Annoyingly, she didn't tell us that much." Kidd thought for a moment. "I want to be looking into Nina's banking records if we can, try and follow the money. If she was borrowing money from someone, then I want to know who and where."

"She was walking around with cash," Janya said. "Surely someone was paying her in cash."

Kidd hesitated. "It's still worth a look," he said. "I need to go and catch up with Weaver. See what he wants us to do next. I can feel a press conference looming, and I really don't like the sound of that."

As anticipated, Weaver was not particularly happy. He was on the phone when Kidd walked into his office, and his mobile phone was vibrating so much he had to turn it off entirely while they talked about what they'd found, where they were going to go from here. It was some comfort to know, at least, that Weaver seemed just as dumbstruck by this as Kidd was.

"These things take time," Kidd said. "We are just over twenty-four hours into this."

"We are," Weaver replied. "And the more time goes by, the less likely we are to find the culprit."

"Give it time," Kidd replied. "Don't count us out just yet."

"The little press conference you gave yesterday was good for holding them over," Weaver said. "They may want us to do something more formal at some point, Let me see what Superintendent Charles says."

"Please don't see what Superintendent Charles says."

"Kidd—"

"Boss, please," Kidd said. "We can figure this out."

"We'll pop a little appeal out for any information we can gather," Weaver said. "Not too much, name of the victims, appeal for witnesses, that kind of thing. Hopefully, it gets them off Diane's back for a little while."

"They're still on Diane's back?"

"They have calmed down some, but I think she still wants to reach down the phone and throttle most of them," Weaver said. "You give them one piece of information, and they'll always come digging for more. You know what those people are like. Insatiable appetites, the lot of them."

"We just need time," Kidd said. "I know we don't have an awful lot of it right now, but I just need you to trust me."

Kidd watched as hesitation drifted across Weaver's face. Maybe there was a small part of him that thought Kidd had lost his knack while he'd been away, that maybe he wasn't the detective he used to be.

He let out a breath, a heavy sigh, one that spoke to the weight of the world being on the DCI's shoulders.

"Fine," he said. "I'll buy you time if I can. No guarantees."

BACK IN THE INCIDENT ROOM, KIDD TASKED HIS TEAM with keeping things moving. He needed to clear his head; he needed to get out of there.

"You okay?" Sanchez asked. "You don't look so good."

"Thanks, Zoe, really kind of you."

"You look freaked."

"Because I am," Kidd said. "I feel like I'm running out of places to turn." He looked at the evidence board, saw the picture of Blake Glover, the guy who worked with Nina.

"Can you chase up Blake Glover for me?" Kidd asked.

"Sure thing, boss," Zoe said. "You want me to come with you?"

"No," he said. "Just give me a moment. I'll be back."

Kidd made his way out of the station, heading for a walk down the riverside to take in the first crime scene once again. It hadn't yet been overrun by people, but there were a couple of bouquets underneath the bridge where Nina had been found. It was sweet. There was a little picture of her there, all smiley and happy. It broke Kidd's heart.

He turned to the restaurants along the seafront, looking to see where the cameras were positioned. It was in plain sight. Once they had the CCTV, they would surely have video footage of Nina being attacked and left there. Why would someone want to be seen? With Harper also being killed, it had to have been some kind of warning. Who was it for? Them? If so, who was trying to get their attention? And why?

Kidd's blood ran cold at the thought. If it was a warning, that would mean that something bigger was at play. And he wasn't sure if he was equipped to deal with that. He would have to be. No time for self-doubt, only time for results.

"How on earth did I know I'd find you here?"

Kidd froze at the familiar voice behind him. The morning had been so busy he'd managed to put it out of his mind, even just for a little while. But now he was being faced with the truth, and it was a truth he did not want to hear.

Kidd turned around and found himself face-to-face with Craig Peyton once again.

"Either because I'm really predictable," Kidd started. "Or because you're stalking me. Don't tell me which, I'm not a fan of either outcome if I'm honest."

There was space between them, like Craig didn't want to close the gap. Kidd certainly didn't want to. Where Craig went, trouble seemed to follow, and he could do without any more trouble, especially from Craig or those connected to him.

"What are you doing here?" Kidd asked.

"Hardly the kind of greeting I was hoping for."

"Welcome back. What are you doing here?" Kidd repeated.

Craig smiled. He really did have a lovely smile, a winning smile, the kind of smile that, once upon a time, Kidd couldn't resist. But those days were long gone. Too much had changed, too much had come between them.

"I... I needed to come back," he said. "I have some things I need to close, loose ends to tie up, things that I didn't get to finish the last time I was here. Billy is doing well."

"Glad to hear it."

"I heard you burned down his boat."

"He lied to you then," Kidd replied with a chuckle. "He got into some trouble. The boat burning was a result of that. I was caught in the crossfire."

"Aren't you always?"

"It seems to be my lot in life, yes," Kidd replied. "You didn't tell me what you were doing here."

"Yes I did."

"You left out the specifics."

"I think it's probably for the best that you don't know," Craig replied. "I don't want you feeling like you have to get involved, or that you have to dive in and save me or anything like that."

"It's not stopped me before."

"Well, quite," Craig said. "That hero complex can't be stopped, can it?" Craig paused, looking down at the flowers and then back up at Kidd. "I heard about what happened to Nina Hawkins."

"Well, it's been pretty well publicised so far," Kidd said. "Makes sense that I'd be involved; I seem to be where the trouble is."

"We have that in common."

Kidd hesitated. He didn't like this, didn't like the easy way that Craig was talking to him, how casual he was being. It made him feel like he was up to something. There was no reason for him to just come back. Why would he come back? He was supposed to be gone for good, wasn't he?

"Shame for The Snake Pit," Craig said. "There was a notice on the door when I walked past. Temporarily closed."

"Well, we had to do something," Kidd said. "We have to come down hard and step in. Can't just have pubs and clubs in Kingston doing whatever the fuck they like and people getting hurt."

"Queens Arms is still going, isn't it?" Craig said with a smirk.

Kidd tensed. "Why are you mentioning The Queen's Arms?" He knew it was one of Andrea's pubs, or her husband's. He had gone there when he was trying to protect Craig the last time he was here, when he'd gone out of his way and put himself in danger just to keep Craig safe. Thinking of it now, it felt stupid. He didn't know what the fuck he'd been playing at.

"I'm making conversation," Craig said with a shrug.

"It feels like you're trying to bait me," Kidd replied

"You're too bloody sensitive," Craig said. "You always were. You know how these places can be sometimes, that's all I'm saying. You never know who's lurking in the corners of these bars. You saw things at The Queen's Arms, and I'm sure while you were down in Southend, you saw all sorts of shady goings on."

Kidd wanted to ask more questions. He wanted to know if Craig knew more about this than he was letting on. Had Nina been working for Andrea? Did he know anything about Harper Gwynn? If all of this was just another connection to Andrea, as if nothing in his life could be anything but a connection to Craig and Andrea and the scheming and the lying and—

"I've missed you," Craig said. "It's nice to see that you're okay."

"What do you mean?" Kidd asked.

"Well, you said you were going away, taking some time out," Craig said. "I know that isn't the kind of thing that you do normally, and I got a little bit worried. I'm glad I got to see you while I am here so that I can see you're doing okay. You're looking well."

"Thanks," Kidd said. "So are you. Apparently, being on the run agrees with you."

Craig snorted. "I've not been on the run," he said. "I disappeared, safe in the knowledge that I didn't have to be on the run. Thank you for that, by the way. I was just choosing to keep a low profile, so that Andrea didn't bump me off."

"A nice way of putting it," Kidd said. "It's dangerous for you to be here, Craig."

"I know."

"She's got worse since you've been gone," Kidd said, barrelling on like Craig hadn't said anything. "Sanchez has been dealing with it mostly. I've just shown up again and feel like I'm being thrown back in the deep end."

"She was never going to quit, you must know that," Craig said. "She's like a hydra, cut off one head and two more grow. Even if you managed to lock her up for it, it's never going to be over."

"Have to burn the whole thing to the ground," Kidd replied.

"Something like that."

Kidd's phone buzzed in his pocket. He took it out to see Zoe's name across the front of the screen. He looked at Craig. "I need to take this."

"It's okay," Craig replied. "I'll probably see you around."

"You probably shouldn't," Kidd replied.

Craig shrugged. "Try and stop me."

Kidd answered the phone, watching as Craig walked away, back up the stairs and onto Kingston

Bridge. He hated the hold that Craig had over him, hated that even the sight of him was enough to send his brain for a loop.

"Hello," Kidd said. "What's up? Do you have Blake? I'm on my way back."

"Wasn't calling to chase you, boss. I've not got hold of Blake yet," Zoe said. "Just got a call with details of Nina's bank transactions. Interesting stuff, and I'm not being sarcastic. Thought you'd want to be here to see it." In his mind's eye, Kidd could see her face wrinkling in concern. "Everything okay?"

"Sure, why wouldn't it be?"

"You sound, I don't know, stressed."

Kidd sighed. "Dead body, Sanchez, bound to be feeling the pressure a little bit," he replied. "I'll be five minutes."

He hung up the phone and looked back to where Craig had been a couple of minutes ago. He was long gone now, somewhere in town, doing goodness knew what; walking into more trouble, no doubt. The thought of it was enough to have his heart racing. He hated it. He hated everything about it. But he had a job to do. He needed to get back to the station.

CHAPTER
TWENTY-ONE

"Say that to me again," Kidd said.

"Everything in the bank account is pretty much as we expected it to be," Powell said. "She was completely broke, for the most part. Every month, she would get a payment from her job at Perkins. Not a huge amount of money, but enough to pull her out of her debt, even temporarily. And then it would just dwindle. She didn't have a good track record with spending."

"Where was it being spent?"

"Some of it at supermarkets, clothes shops, that kind of thing," Powell said. "The rest of it was going to bars and clubs, The Snake Pit being one of them. And then the rest seemed to be going to pay off credit cards, the ones that she has absolutely maxed out." He took a moment. "But there are a couple of big payments over the past six months that have been... interesting."

"Okay."

"They're the ones that I think we're going to need to dig into," Powell said. "They're all coming from the same account, huge payments of hundreds of pounds at a time, sometimes thousands."

"And what is she doing with that?"

"Pretty much a combination of what was being done previously," Powell said. "The food shop, the clubs, paying off the other debts. Someone was sending money to her."

"And it wasn't cash deposits?" Kidd asked, thinking about the wad of cash that had been found in her purse.

"No, these were all bank transfers," Powell said. "It's all from the same place, from the same person. If you go back to the middle of last year, this person has been steadily sending thousands of pounds, and I really do mean thousands," Powell continued. "It was barely pulling her out of whatever problems she was getting herself into. Or the money was there one minute and then she'd spent it on something the next, her finances were a mess."

"And she just kept borrowing?"

"She couldn't seem to keep a lid on it," Powell said. "And we know that when people get into situations like that, they can get desperate, and when people get desperate, they get stupid." Powell paused. "If Nina had fallen in with a bad crowd, then the person at the end of this series of numbers could be the person who killed her."

Kidd thought about it for a second. She clearly wasn't paying the money back, just getting herself into more and more debt with this person. Was it possible that they'd finally cut her off? Had they asked to be paid back? Was it all getting to be too much?

"When did the payments stop?" Kidd asked.

"The last one was about six weeks ago," Powell said. "There hasn't been one for the past six weeks, and her finances have seriously dwindled. Christ knows what she was going to do, but this person had just stopped paying her."

"Six weeks ago was when she went to her father asking for money," Zoe said.

"My thoughts exactly," Kidd said. "So whoever this is, it's likely that they were starting to demand repayment, and... and she went to the only people that she thought would be able to help—her parents —and they didn't help her. They basically signed her death warrant."

"Fucking hell," Sanchez breathed.

"We need to know who this person is, and we need to know now," Kidd barked. "Who is on that?"

Ash raised his hand from his desk. He had a phone in one hand and was tapping away on his computer as they spoke. Kidd had to believe he was on it, that he was making progress.

Was this about to lead them straight to Andrea's door? Was this about to give them something else to add to the list of things that were currently being investigated elsewhere in this very building? He held his breath as he waited.

Ash hung up the phone.

"Got it," he said.

It was go time.

CHAPTER
TWENTY-TWO

"This is really what you want to do?" Weaver asked, sitting back in his chair, eyeing Kidd carefully. "We have no proof he had anything to do with Nina's death, how involved he is—"

"He has been putting money into the girl's account for the past six months, and the second it stops is the second she goes to her parents needing help," Kidd said. "That doesn't sound like a coincidence to me. Does it sound like one to you?"

Weaver hesitated for a moment. He clearly didn't like the sound of this, didn't like where this was going, but this was, as far as Kidd was concerned, the strongest piece of evidence they had so far. They couldn't hesitate, they needed to act before he knew that they were onto him.

"Who is this person?"

"Dwight Griffith," Kidd said. "We've done a little

background check on him and, I'll be honest, we've not come up with much."

"No criminal record?" Weaver asked.

"Pretty crimes," Kidd replied. "So we've got a visual on him at least, an address, that kind of thing. But nothing major."

"But you still think he's responsible?"

"It's his bank account, sir," Kidd said. "And if he's been sending her that money, then he knows something. We've put out an appeal, we've put out her name, and he has yet to come forward. He knows her, and he knows he has something to hide."

"Kidd, this is a big swing."

"And one worth taking, I would say," Kidd replied. "I need you to back me on this, boss. We have an address, we can get ourselves over there now, and we can put an end to this before we add to the body count. We've lost Nina and now we've lost Harper. We can't lose another one."

Weaver was still hesitating. There was something stopping him, and Kidd once again had that horrible feeling that Weaver didn't quite trust him anymore. It was sobering. Horribly sobering.

"Boss?"

"I'll set it up," Weaver said. "I'll get uniforms to check on the address. They won't approach. They'll just make sure our man is there."

"Sounds good."

"Do we have any CCTV from The Snake Pit yet?"

"Not yet, boss."

"Okay," Weaver said. "So all we have are the bank transfers to Nina Hawkins."

"Totalling somewhere in the region of seven thousand pounds, sir," Kidd said, throwing the figure in there, trying to add gravity to the situation.

"Okay then," Weaver said. "I will put in all the necessary calls, and you can get ready for tonight. Put a briefing together, run it by me. We will do this as soon as we can confirm he is at the property."

"Sounds like a plan," Kidd said. He was about to get up from his chair when something about how Weaver was looking at him gave him pause. "Problem?"

"Not at all," Weaver replied. "Just want to check in and make sure you're okay."

"Why wouldn't I be okay?"

"First case back, Kidd, this is me trying to be a good boss; don't make it a big deal," Weaver said, his voice coming out gruff, almost like he was embarrassed. "How is it going?"

"Well, it's my first case back here, but not the first case I've done since I left."

"I know, Kidd," Weaver replied. "But you're back here for the first time in a while, and there are a lot of memories here, ghosts and such. I just want to make sure that you're okay, and that, if you're not, I'm doing all I can to make sure you're getting the help you need."

Kidd smiled at him. DCI Patrick Weaver was not one for displays of affection or kindness. He was very by the book, very hard-lined, so this was practically a hug. He didn't want to make a big deal out of it, but he also didn't want it to go entirely unacknowledged.

"Thank you, sir, I appreciate that," Kidd replied. "Everything is good for the time being. We're making progress, decent enough headway with this case. We'll... We'll see what this brings."

<hr />

THE DAY WORE ON SLOWLY AS THEY GATHERED THE rest of their information, as they waited for confirmation that Dwight wasn't leaving the house. There had been no one going in or out all day, the car that was registered to him remaining on the driveway.

Once Weaver had the relevant warrants, once everything was in place, they travelled over to the address with the firearms officers. The entire team was in tow, no one wanting to miss it. Kidd could feel the pressure piled onto his chest, the kind of pressure that made it difficult to breathe, that told him just how much of a big deal this was, how he wasn't wholly sure how this was going to turn out.

There were no blue lights, there were no sirens, there was nothing to make this look like a raid in any way. They needed to be as stealthy as possible. They didn't want to give him a chance to run, they couldn't afford to lose him.

Kidd and the team waited while the armed officers fanned out around the house, while they positioned themselves around the back and front, covering any and all exits.

And then it felt like the entire world exploded around Kidd. The door was caved in, the sounds of officers screaming "GET BACK! GET BACK!" filling the air around him and pouring out into the cul-de-sac.

He saw people start to come out of their houses, piling out to see what the commotion was about. Uniformed officers were already on hand to do exactly what the armed officers inside were yelling, telling everyone to get back.

Kidd held his breath, waiting for Dwight Griffith to be brought out in handcuffs, to be taken back to the squad car, to be brought into the police station for questioning, for DNA swabbing, to start the process of proving that he was the one who had murdered Nina Hawkins and Harper Gwynn.

An officer appeared at the door. He nodded to Kidd, and he felt his stomach drop out from inside him. Something was wrong. Or at the very least, something wasn't right.

Kidd made his way towards the house, crossing the threshold and being hit with a far too familiar scent, a metallic smell that sent his mind back to all sorts of cases in the past, the bloodier cases, the ones that imprinted on his mind like no others.

The closer he got to the room, the worse the smell became, not just the smell of blood but the smell of decay, the smell of a dead body as it slowly putrefied. Kidd was struggling to hold on to the contents of his stomach. He could hardly bear it.

He followed the arms officer to the living room, where he saw Dwight Griffith lying in a pool of his blood.

CHAPTER
TWENTY-THREE

K idd immediately felt sick at the sight of it. It wasn't what he'd hoped for, wasn't what he'd planned for, but there he was. His face was the same one they had in their police files, maybe a little more drawn than it had been before, maybe a little older, definitely a heck of a lot paler.

There were signs of a struggle in the room. There were things that had been knocked onto the floor and smashed—a vase of dead flowers, a picture frame that had been smashed. The blood that had spattered onto the carpet had sunk in, leaving deep red pools around him. How long had he been like this? Based on the smell, based on the way his body looked, it had to have been a couple of days. He didn't look fresh, he certainly didn't smell fresh.

No wonder the car hadn't gone anywhere all day.

It was a wonder the neighbours hadn't started to smell him. It truly was an assault on the senses.

"Not what we were hoping for," Weaver said as he joined Kidd in the living room, staring down at the body. He looked green like he was about to lose his lunch. Kidd wasn't feeling quite so hot himself. He signalled for the two of them to leave.

The arms officers were making their way away from the scene, a couple of uniforms already setting up a cordon at DS Sanchez's say-so.

"Fuck's sake," Kidd growled. "This is... This isn't good, sir. I can't put it any other way. This was my lead."

"I know, Kidd."

He started to run through things in his head, trying to figure out what could have happened, trying to piece together some kind of timeline. What connected Nina to Dwight was the money being transferred. That could have been enough to tie him to her death, but now...

"What are you thinking, Kidd?" Weaver asked.

"I'm not sure, sir," Kidd said. "I'm really not sure."

Weaver nodded. "Back to the station," he said. "Forensics will get us reports. Come on now."

BACK AT THE STATION, THINGS DIDN'T FEEL MUCH better. They debriefed on what they'd found, and added Dwight to the list of bodies on the board. Then Weaver arrived to tell them to call it a day, sending the team home, telling them to come back to it tomorrow with fresh eyes.

"That goes for you too, Kidd," he said. "I can't have you totally fucked for tomorrow. Get yourself out of here."

"It might not even be connected," Kidd said.

"What's that?"

"This guy, if he's the guy that Harper was describing, was some kind of loan shark," Kidd said. "There could be any number of people who were after him."

"Or it is all connected because this person is connected to Nina and therefore connected to Harper," Weaver said. "We can't rule anything out at this stage, Kidd. We need to keep our eyes open and keep moving forward."

But all Kidd could think about was how much hope he had pinned on this find, how certain he had been that this was going to amount to something. And now, here he was without it, entirely unsure what he was supposed to do next.

Andrea. Craig. Nina. Harper. Dwight. They still needed to speak to the people that Nina worked with at Perkins, see if there was anything there. Maybe they needed to speak to her friends again. They'd not said a word to them about Harper. What did that mean? Why hadn't they told them about Harper Gwynn?

"Kidd, you're going to drive yourself nuts if you stay here," Weaver said before turning his attention to Sanchez. "Make sure he goes home. I don't want to come back tomorrow morning and find him sleeping behind that desk."

"I won't leave the building without him."

"And that goes for you too," Weaver said. "I know what a bad influence he's been on you. Don't let him ruin your sleep too."

Weaver left the Incident Room, leaving the two of them waiting in silence. Kidd felt lost. Sanchez grabbed him by the arm, practically dragging him to the door.

"Come on," she said. "I'm not getting in trouble with Hurricane Weaver because of you. Let's go."

Kidd and Sanchez made their way out of the station, the night dark around them, everything feeling more than a little bit hopeless, at least as far as Kidd was concerned.

What the fuck had happened? How had things gotten so mixed up, so bloody quickly?

They stepped out into the cold night air, the sobering shot of Baltic air filling Kidd's lungs.

"I've not seen you this spooked in a long time," Zoe said. "What's going on? Is it the Andrea situation? Because you can talk to me about that. I'm in the loop now. I know things."

"I know you know things."

"So what are you keeping from me?" She asked.

"Come on, Kidd, after what happened last time with all that shit with Andrea, we can't be keeping secrets from one another, not anymore."

Kidd stopped and sighed. There was no use in keeping it from her. Otherwise, she would find out eventually, and that would just be a million times worse.

"Fucking hell, what?" she asked, voice laced with panic. "What are you keeping from me?"

"Okay, I haven't been keeping it from you," Kidd said. "This is a recent development and not one that is welcome; I feel the need to make sure you know that."

"What?"

"Craig is back."

Zoe's face dropped. "You're fucking joking."

"I wouldn't joke about that," Kidd said. "Please, I wouldn't dream of it."

Zoe eyed him carefully. She knew about his relationship with Craig, the turbulence of it all, and that when it all came down to it, Kidd would do anything to help Craig. He knew it wasn't healthy, so did she, but they weren't about to fall out over it.

"He appeared last night, and I was pretty sure I was imagining it," Kidd said. "We had contact a bit before I left, and then there was the guy down in Southend who was connected to all of this, and I had to call him to ask him things for you, remember? I thought he was done with Kingston, done with Andrea."

"Is he not in massive amounts of danger being back here with Andrea floating about?"

"That's what I said."

"So you've spoken to him?" Zoe asked.

"I went to look at the crime scene," Kidd said. "I'd actually planned to go and get some food, but then I got distracted by that, and then Craig. Then you called, so I came back."

"You need to eat something."

"Okay, Mum, it's home-time now, I'll order in when I get back."

"Promise?"

"Promise."

"What did Craig say?"

Kidd sighed. "He said he was tying up loose ends," he replied.

"So, nice and vague."

"Exactly," Kidd replied. "Makes me nervous, because I have no idea what he's about to do. But he seems to know something about what's been going on here."

"With Nina?"

"Yeah," Kidd replied. "He was pretty vague, as you might expect, but he mentioned shady characters at venues and how things go down in clubs. He mentioned The Queens Arms, all of that shit."

"Christ," Zoe said. "So things just keep getting more and more complicated."

"It would seem so," Kidd replied. "I need to talk to John about it when I get home."

Zoe winced.

"What?"

"You're sure that's a good idea?"

"Yes," Kidd said. "Keeping things from him about Craig has never served me well in the past. At the very least, he deserves to know that he's shown up again. And that I'm going to need to talk to him."

"That was going to be my next point," Zoe said. "If Craig knows stuff, we may need to bring him in for a chat."

"If we bring him in for a chat and Weaver gets wind of it, he might pull me off the case," Kidd replied. "Conflict of interest and all that."

"Then just talk to him," Zoe said. "See if he can maybe point us in the right direction. Every little bit helps."

"True enough," Kidd replied.

They carried on walking, Kidd dropping Zoe off at her house before he made his way to his own. He could feel himself dragging his feet every step of the way. This was not going to be a happy conversation, but he needed to have it. And quickly. Rip off the plaster.

They'd had several conversations about Craig over the course of their relationship, to varying degrees of success. Kidd didn't want to rock the boat, not really. They'd just come back from their little jaunt around the UK, and things felt like they were clicking along quite nicely. But if he kept it from him, he knew it would blow up in his face.

If there was one thing that was entirely certain in Kidd's life, it was that secrets had a habit of coming out, no matter how well you thought you'd hidden them. He didn't want to keep things from John. He didn't want to ruin things.

He hung his jacket up and made his way through to the kitchen, putting on the kettle for a cup of tea. John would be home soon, having been in the office today, and he wanted a little bit of time to steady himself before he broke the news. Tea would help. Tea always helped.

"Evening!" John called out as he stepped into the house, the door closing with a slam behind him. "I think we need to go away again. I'm already sick of being back in the office. I also think I'm going to need to go to my flat and pick up some more things because I'm here all the time."

"Do you need help?"

"I'll swing by on my way back from work tomorrow," he said. "How was your day?"

"Eventful," Kidd replied, heading into the kitchen.

John was taking off his coat, dropping his bag on the floor. Kidd could see the weight of the day on him. He wasn't enjoying his back-to-office life, and Kidd couldn't blame him. John's work sounded like just as much of a nightmare as his. Just with less death. Any death he had to deal with was written on the page.

"Tea?"

"God, yes," John said. "Order in for dinner?"

"You read my mind," Kidd replied.

"I'll do it before I take a shower, then it will probably be here by the time I'm done," he said, stepping into the kitchen and giving Kidd a quick kiss. "You seem tense."

"I'm always tense."

"I know you're always tense. I just mean more tense than normal," John replied. "What's going on? Your day that bad?"

There wasn't going to be an easy way to say it, no way to tell him that would soften the blow. He needed to tear it off like a plaster.

"I saw Craig today," Kidd said.

John stepped away from him, eyes narrowed, face twisted in confusion, and Kidd suddenly realised it required more explanation than that because, as far as John was aware, Craig had vanished several months ago, never to be seen or heard from again.

"He just showed up," Kidd said. "I thought I saw him last night when we were outside The Snake Pit, but figured it was just me seeing things, but... then he just appeared."

"That explains why you didn't sleep last night," John said. "You can't be okay with all that going on."

"Not one bit," Kidd replied. "But I wanted to tell you, because if I didn't tell you, he'd end up showing up unannounced somewhere and then I'd have some serious explaining to do."

"Smart," John replied. "So you saw him."

"He sort of crept up on me while I was at a crime scene," Kidd replied. "And... well... he said he's back here to tie up some loose ends. Unfinished business and all that."

"Sounds like he's in trouble."

"My thoughts exactly."

"Sounds like you need to keep away from it if you can," John said, but something on Kidd's face gave him away. "But you're not going to do that, are you?"

"He's tying up loose ends and... I don't know, something about that concerns me."

"Okay."

"And he knows things about Nina—the first victim—and the pubs and clubs in Kingston."

John raised an eyebrow. "Do you think he might be involved?"

"No," Kidd replied, though he wasn't sure if it was that he didn't believe it or that he didn't want to believe it. "But he knows things, and the connection with Andrea means he may have some vital information."

"So you're going to be talking to him about this case at some point?"

Kidd hesitated. He didn't really want to pull Craig into this case, because it raised more questions with Weaver than he would like. But he also knew that Craig could potentially be helpful. He was caught.

"I don't know," Kidd said. "But I wanted to tell you because I wanted you to know that you have nothing to worry about. I didn't want you to be blindsided."

John nodded. "I feel pretty blindsided by you telling me, to be honest," he said. "But I'm glad you did. That's something, at least."

He took a breath, running a hand through his hair. The kettle boiled, clicking off, sending steam up into the air around them, bathing them in silence, neither one of them sure what to say next.

"I know you're telling me that I have nothing to worry about," John started. "And I want to believe you, it's just that whenever something comes up around Craig, you always seem to go out of your way to help and end up getting caught in the crossfire."

"I know."

"And that makes me worry," John said. "I'm always going to worry when it comes to Craig Peyton."

Kidd nodded. "I understand that."

"What do you want for dinner?"

Kidd blinked. "What?"

"I said I was going to order dinner and take a shower, and I'm hungry, so... What do you want for dinner?"

The conversation was over. John had said his piece, and that was that. Kidd didn't mind that they were done talking about it, but he did mind that John would worry. He didn't want that.

"Whatever," Kidd said. "I'm easy, whatever you want."

"Okay," John said. "I'll order it and be down in a bit."

He watched as John walked away, listening to him as he went upstairs and into the bathroom. The silence made Kidd feel uncomfortable, and he wondered whether he'd done the right thing. It was one thing for him to be worried about Craig being back and what his involvement was in the case, but he didn't want John worrying about that too.

Too late for that, he thought, pulling two mugs out of the cupboard. Far too late for that.

CHAPTER
TWENTY-FOUR

They spent their evening dancing around the subject as best they could. Kidd could feel the presence of it in the room, like it was always there, lingering in the corner, trying to push its way into the conversation, but they just ignored it.

Kidd didn't know if John was feeling it too, but the tension was almost too much for Kidd to deal with. He just wanted to talk about it, wanted to reassure John that things were going to be okay, that Craig showing up again didn't impact the two of them at all. But he knew that he couldn't make that promise. Because whenever Craig showed up, or even the idea of Craig showed up, there always seemed to be something.

John tidied up after they had dinner, washing up the plates, the glasses, wiping down the countertops.

Kidd dried everything, putting it back in the cupboards, the two of them making the kitchen spotless while the TV continued to play in the background.

"I'm going to head back to mine tonight," John said. "I don't have clothes here for tomorrow. I knew I should have stopped off before I came home."

"You want me to come with you and pick some things up?" Kidd asked.

John smiled. "No, it's okay," he said. "I'll just stay there. It's probably easier that way."

"Okay," Kidd said, not wanting to start an argument, not wanting to cause any issues between them. It was normal for John to spend a couple of days with him and then a couple of days back at his own flat. They were living so in and out of each other's pockets that it was hard to keep track sometimes. But it would be the first time he'd properly been back since they got back from their trip. And that felt significant in ways that Kidd didn't like.

John made his way to the door, grabbing his things and saying goodbye, and Kidd just watched him go, a sick feeling settling in the pit of his stomach.

He knew that he'd done the right thing, and he couldn't blame John for reacting the way he was, but it didn't make it hurt any less that he felt he needed to leave.

Kidd settled back in front of the TV, putting on

something that he'd watched before and just letting it wash over him as the time ticked by in his big, silent house. He was right about one thing, where Craig went, trouble followed. Tonight was the direct result of his return. It hadn't been chaos and fire, it had been quiet and calm. And in a lot of ways, that made it a hundred times worse.

KIDD AWOKE THE FOLLOWING DAY, NOT PARTICULARLY well-rested. He'd fallen asleep on the sofa at some point and steadily made his way upstairs to brush his teeth and throw himself into bed, but he was fitful all night. He kept waking up thinking he'd heard a noise in the house, or wondering where John had got to, and it was enough to stop him from sleeping through the night.

It felt embarrassing to think that a complete non-argument with his partner had resulted in this. He had never been that kind of person. He used to be so good at shutting off those feelings. Not anymore. He'd become more open, and in doing so, had left himself open to this kind of hurt. Those were the pitfalls.

Kidd dragged himself out of bed and forced himself into his running gear. He didn't want to run, it was the last thing he wanted to do, and whenever a case really got going, it was the first thing to go out of the window. But he needed to keep on top of his fitness or he was going to end up with another pain-in-the-arse fitness test that would nearly kill him when the time rolled around.

He took his usual route through town and down by the river. He passed the memorial for Nina Hawkins, the small collection of flowers and tributes had grown a little overnight, and continued along until his legs couldn't carry him any further. He doubled over in front of the river, staring out at it, knowing there were no answers on the water, but at least there was some peace, some tranquillity.

Kidd felt lost as to what to do next. The loan shark that they'd been so certain would be at the centre of all of this was dead, brutally murdered, and they had two other bodies that had been strangled to death. Were they connected? It was hard to say. And if they were, how? There were so many questions swirling around in Kidd's head, it was hard for him to pin any one of them down.

He turned back, walking the same route he'd just run, breathing in the cold, winter air, trying to invigorate himself, waiting for his heart rate to slow post-run. But even once that had faded, he found himself unable to stop the anxious pitter-patter of his heart. Anxiety was a beast, and he was afflicted.

He walked past The Snake Pit, the big closed sign on the front of the double doors, a smaller notice detailing how they hoped to welcome everyone back soon. Kidd hoped so too, because if they were welcoming everyone back, that would mean this investigation was over and that maybe, just maybe, things weren't going to be looking quite so bad.

Kidd made his way back to his house, showered and got himself ready for work, once again having to walk past Nina's memorial just to get to the station. Here was the other problem with living so close to where you worked. Everywhere you went, you were reminded of your case. Even afterwards, there would be things that Kidd saw, recognised, that would take him back to this exact moment. Things in Southend had felt easier. There were fewer ghosts there. Weaver was right.

Never thought I would think that, Kidd thought.

He got to the Incident Room and got himself set up for the day, replying to the emails that had come in overnight, forcing some kind of joy into his voice when he greeted the rest of his team as they entered. They could likely tell that he wasn't all there, that things weren't going so well for him, but they weren't about to question him on it. They were just letting him get on with things, going back to what they had been working on the day before. What had happened yesterday had taken it out of all of them. Maybe they'd all been pinning their hopes on that raid being the key to solving this.

They continued with their work for the morning, phones ringing, calls being made. They were waiting to make their next move, and the lack of action was driving Kidd insane. The worst part was that there was nothing he could do about it.

Kidd's phone rang and he practically jumped on it. "Hello?"

"It's only me," Weaver said. "Sorry, were you expecting someone else?"

"I don't know what I was expecting," Kidd replied. "How are things?"

"Not too great," Weaver replied. "I think we need to set up that press conference for today if we can, maybe later on this afternoon."

"Christ."

"I know it's not an ideal situation, Kidd, but we need to make sure we're appealing for information here," Weaver replied. "Superintendent Charles said—"

"I hate any sentence that starts with that."

"He said," Weaver continued, raising his voice to let Kidd know that he was still talking, that he was the one in control of this conversation, whether he liked it or not. "That we need to be seen to be taking action, to be doing something. And if we are staying silent on this when we have a body count of three, people are going to start answering their own questions."

Another phone in the incident room rang, DC Powell picked it up and immediately seemed to light up. It must have been a personal call.

"And the press are going to be asking us questions that we're not equipped to answer," Kidd replied. "We're walking into the lion's den with nothing to defend ourselves with."

"Take a few questions, appeal for more information, it doesn't have to be anything more serious than that," Weaver said. "I know you hate them. Lord knows I hate them too, but they're a necessary evil and if it keeps them from pissing off Diane or any of the other station officers that work here, then maybe it's a good thing. It will keep them off our backs."

"Or have them breathing down our necks all the more."

"A risk we need to take," Weaver said. "I'm arranging it for this afternoon. Please keep your diary clear. Any excuses to not be there need to come with a coroner's note."

"How cheery."

"What can I say? I'm a barrel of laughs," Weaver deadpanned before hanging up the phone.

Powell hung up the phone and turned his attention squarely on Kidd. He had a strange look on his face, the kind of look that made Kidd feel nervous. He had something to say, and he didn't know how Kidd was going to react to it, that much was clear.

"That was Helene from pathology," Powell said. "She's sending me through the full report now, but you're never going to guess whose DNA was found all over Dwight Griffith's apartment, and all over Dwight."

"Whose?" Kidd asked.

"Nina Hawkins."

It was like someone had pulled a trapdoor from beneath Kidd's feet. What on earth was going on?

CHAPTER
TWENTY-FIVE

"Her DNA was found all over Dwight's body, on the door handles, there were footprints in the blood that we might be able to track to a pair of her shoes, but the footprints were all there," Powell said. "There was even some of her DNA under his fingernails where he'd likely tried to fight back."

"So what do we think happened here?" Kidd asked. It was a general question to the room. He was forming his own theories at the same time, but he wanted to hear what they were all thinking.

"So Nina killed her loan shark," Zoe started. "She was indebted to him for several thousand pounds and had no conceivable way of paying it back. Had he been threatening her? Did we ever find out who sent those notes to her? The ones we found in her bedroom?"

"I was still pretty sure it was going to be someone she worked with up until we saw the bank transactions," Janya said. "But it would make sense that if he was the one who was threatening her, that she... took matters into her own hands."

"It was her or him at the end of the day," Zoe said. "And she decided that it was him. And..." She took a moment, moving to the evidence board, looking at the pictures they had of Nina's dead body, of the purse with all the money in it. "Do we think this money was his?"

"Maybe," Kidd said. "Why would she take it out with her? Isn't that... Isn't that a little bit unhinged?"

"I'd say," Ash piped up. "You can't be wandering around with all that cash."

"But if she had killed the guy, this could be her last connection to him," Zoe said. "What if she was intending to splash all that cash the other night, get rid of it, and then she would totally be free of him?"

"Until someone found the body," Ash said.

"But maybe she'd not thought that far ahead," Kidd said. "She was thinking of the here and the now, and in the here and the now, she needed to get rid of Dwight to protect herself. But in doing so, she unlocked a totally different can of worms because it's very possible that whoever it was that killed Nina had some connection to Dwight."

He looked over at Sanchez, whose eyes widened. They were having the same thought, they both figured that the connection was going to be Andrea, and now that one of her people had been taken out, she was seeking revenge on Nina.

"But why kill Harper?" Powell asked. All eyes turned to Simon. "If someone was after getting revenge on Nina, the only reason to kill Harper would be—"

"Because someone saw her coming to the police station and thought that she had given us some useful information," Kidd said.

"Does that mean this is over?" Ash asked. "If Nina is out of the picture, if Harper, the only other person with information, is out of the picture, is that the end? Does all of this go away?"

"This doesn't go away until I say it does," Kidd said firmly. "Nina might have killed that loan shark, but someone has taken out Nina and Harper, and we need to figure out how on earth that all fits together."

"I've got a thought," Janya said, taking a position next to Zoe at the evidence board. There were pictures of Nina's housemates there: Paige, Sienna, Bailey, all of them staring out from their pictures with broad smiles on their faces, like butter wouldn't melt.

"Go on," Kidd said.

"Well, if her friends all knew that she was having money problems, if they were all having money problems, what if this all went deeper than just Nina?" Janya asked.

"What do you mean?" Kidd asked. "You think they might have been getting money off him too?"

"I don't know about that," Janya said. "But there was a lot of talk of money worries, and a lot of trying to shift the blame elsewhere. I don't know. It might be worth talking to them again."

Kidd nodded. "Go for it. Go and see what you can find out. I am going to get on at Forensics, see if they can't find anything at his house that might point to him writing those threatening notes to Nina. She was in deep trouble and clearly thought this was the only way out."

Zoe swallowed. "Maybe it was," she said. "What she didn't know is that it was going to open up an even bigger can of worms."

DCs Ravel and Hale made their way back to the house they had visited just a couple of days ago. They didn't call ahead this time, didn't give them any warning, just showed up on the doorstep, much to the surprise of Sienna, who was the one to answer the door this time around.

She looked like she'd been crying, eyes red, face puffy. It wasn't how she had been just a couple of days ago. A couple of days ago, she had seemed absolutely fine, like she wasn't that bothered about what had happened. What had changed?

"Sorry," she said as she answered the door, wiping the tears from her face. "I... I wasn't expecting you."

"I know," Janya replied. "May we come in? We had a few follow-up questions for you and Paige, if she's around."

Sienna nodded. "She's around. She's not gone back to work yet. Neither of us has."

She opened the door and ushered them inside. The house was a lot fuller than it had been when they'd first been here. Bailey McBride was sitting on an armchair, curled up beneath a blanket with a cup of tea. She was dressed head to toe in black, with dyed black hair messy around her face, like she was trying to disappear into it, as well as the blanket. She turned the TV off when the detectives stepped inside. And there was a new face. One that Janya and Ash hadn't seen before, not even in pictures.

"We've not been introduced," Janya said. "Detective Constable Janya Ravel, this is my colleague, DC Ashley Hale. You are?"

"Maggie Parks," the girl said. She was sitting on the arm of the sofa, Sienna parking herself on the sofa next to her. Now that they were sitting side by side, Janya could see the resemblance, the same dark hair, the same perfect skin, the same slightly sneery expression. "Sienna is my sister. When everything started kicking off, I thought it wise for me to come down and make sure she was okay."

"She clearly isn't," Janya said with a soft smile. "You're a good sister."

Maggie smiled. "I certainly try my best."

Janya turned her attention back to Sienna. "Is Paige here?"

"I'll go get her," Bailey said, getting to her feet. There was a slight monotone to her voice, like she was already bored by them being there, interrupting whatever show she had been watching. She disappeared from the room, reappearing a couple of minutes later with Paige in tow. She looked a lot more put together than she had done a couple of days ago. She had swapped places with Sienna emotionally. Paige looked like a new woman. It was Sienna's turn to be falling apart.

"Is everything okay?" Paige asked. "I didn't think we'd be seeing you again."

"I'm not sure how much you would have seen of this," Janya said. "Or if you've been keeping up with the news surrounding Nina's case, but we found another body yesterday morning." The entire room seemed to be holding its breath, the air suddenly feeling thick, soupy. "Harper Gwynn was found strangled to death in her apartment."

"Jesus Christ," Sienna breathed, tears starting to flow once again. Her sister wrapped an arm around her shoulder, shushing her, trying to comfort her as she started to cry.

"You're joking," Paige said. "What did... How did... I'm sorry, this is just a little out of the blue."

"We could say the same," Janya said. "We hadn't even heard the name Harper Gwynn until she came to the station the day before last to give us some information about Nina. She was her girlfriend, wasn't she?"

"Ex-girlfriend," Bailey corrected.

"Semantics," Janya replied. "Why was she not mentioned at all when we spoke the other day?"

"We didn't think it was relevant," Paige said. "They broke up months ago, I didn't think that they were even still in contact, it didn't feel like the kind of thing we needed to be talking to you about. It didn't feel worth dragging her into it."

"She seemed to do a pretty good job of making sure she was involved anyway," Bailey said. "She had a way of sticking her nose in where it wasn't wanted. And here she has again. She didn't have anything to do with Nina anymore, and yet she still was trying to muscle in on her life."

There was clearly no love lost for Harper Gwynn in this room. Something had obviously happened between them and Harper at some point, but no one was being particularly forthcoming about what it was. Janya wasn't altogether sure she was even interested. She didn't need to be involved in petty dramas, she needed to get down to what had happened here.

And she needed to know exactly what they knew about Dwight Griffith.

"We talked about Nina's financial worries," Janya said. "I think both Paige and Sienna, you mentioned that you struggled for money sometimes too, but Nina had it hardest."

Maggie turned her attention sharply to her sister. "You've been struggling for money?" she asked. "Why didn't you say something?"

"It doesn't matter," Sienna replied, colour rushing to her cheeks. "It's all fine."

"Does the name Dwight Griffith mean anything to you?" Janya asked. She watched them all in turn, waited as the name settled in the room, as the clear recognition for the name rippled through them all. "I'll take that as a yes."

"She got desperate," Paige said quickly.

"Paige!" Sienna barked.

"What, Sienna? There's no point in hiding it now," she said.

"You could get us into some serious trouble; that's a reason," Sienna snapped. The sadness had faded, quickly replaced by outright anger. It had clearly rubbed Sienna up the wrong way.

"Paige is right," Ash said, looking up from the notes he had been taking. "There is no point in hiding it now, given that we know he was loaning money to Nina. And if you all knew about it, you could have saved us a lot of trouble when it came to finding this out, finding someone else we could talk to with a connection to Nina."

"There's been an awful lot of secrets floating around this room, it makes me wonder what else you might be hiding," Janya said, allowing the words to hang in the air for a little while.

"We were scared," Sienna said. "We knew... We knew what he was like."

"How?" Janya asked.

"We'd all borrowed from him," Sienna said. "We all needed money, we all borrowed from him, we all knew how dangerous he was. It was just... Nina, who kept going back, kept asking for more and more because she was the one who needed it most and now..."

"You think Dwight killed her?" Janya asked.

Sienna nodded. Bailey nodded. Paige didn't. Paige stayed where she was in the door frame, like she might be about to bolt in the opposite direction.

"Paige?" Janya pressed.

"I don't think that," she said. "Because Nina killed him."

CHAPTER
TWENTY-SIX

Kidd and Sanchez made their way back down to the crime scene of Dwight Griffith's house. They said their hellos to the officers on the cordon, and made their way into the property, shoes covered, hands gloved. They didn't know what they were looking for, just that they needed to be looking for something.

A lot of things had been bagged up by the forensic team, things that were mostly from the living room. They'd not made their way through the rest of the house. Kidd wanted to check on things, see if he could find handwriting that matched what was on the notes they'd found in Nina's desk, see if he could find anything that might point to who he was working for, if anyone.

"You think he was working for Andrea?" Zoe asked.

"I don't know," Kidd said. "That's what I want to figure out."

"Why?"

"Because if he's working for Andrea, we'll need to hand this over," Kidd said. "We'd be putting ourselves in danger by even continuing to look into this if she has anything to do with it."

"She really has you spooked, doesn't she?"

"Does she not you?"

"She does," Zoe replied. "It's just... I'm used to seeing you a little more fearless than all of this, Ben. Are you sure you're okay to be doing this?"

Kidd paused in the hallway, looking up the stairs of Dwight's house. He wasn't sure he should be doing it, wasn't sure he should have even come back here, to Kingston, to the job, but here he was. He couldn't turn back.

"Nope," he replied before starting up the stairs and into the darkened house. He turned on the lights, the sun outside not quite managing to penetrate the hallway upstairs, the closed doors. He tried the first door, the bathroom. It was clean, empty, nothing there of interest.

He tried the next room along the corridor. It wasn't the main bedroom, looked more like a spare room than anything else. It was decorated in soft pinks, the bed was made, everything about it looked like it hadn't been touched in a while. He could smell the dust in the air. There was no use wasting any more time.

Kidd started working his way through the drawers as Zoe started on the wardrobe, under the bed, any sort of storage box looking for... something. Anything.

They moved to the next room, an office that was clearly well-used. There were papers all over the desk, strewn haphazardly across it. Kidd started riffling through them, looking at bills, advertisements, flyers, while Zoe looked through the stack of notebooks on the shelves.

"Ben," she said. Kidd looked up. She nodded him over, showing him the open pages of a notebook. It looked like a diary, a personal journal. The handwriting was spidery, like it had been done without much care, maybe in a hurry.

Kidd reached into his pocket and pulled out one of the notes that had been left in Nina's bedroom when Janya and Ash had gone to take a look. He looked for specific letters, checking the vowels, making sure they were the same or similar, similar enough. He flicked to a few more pages, checked a few more letters, seeing if they corresponded.

"How does that look to you?" Kidd asked. It wasn't that he didn't trust his own judgment, he just wanted to make sure that his desperation in wanting to find something didn't have him seeing what wasn't really there.

"That looks like it might be his writing," Zoe said. "There are more of them," she added. "We can keep looking."

"Bag them up," Kidd said, going back to the desk and rummaging through the drawers. "We can have them checked properly, but it looks like that closes the circle on Nina and Dwight to me."

"He was threatening her, so she killed him?"

"It certainly seems that way," Kidd said.

"Then the question becomes who the fuck killed Nina?"

"Exactly," Kidd replied. "Come on, still another couple of rooms to check through."

They made their way to another spare bedroom and then to the main bedroom. It was huge, twice the size of the spare rooms they'd seen so far, and it had clearly been lived in. There was a glass on the dressing table, a mug with tea stains around the rim just next to it. There was a pair of glasses on there too, sitting on top of a hardback with the dust jacket taken off.

Zoe went to the wardrobe, Kidd started at the bedside tables, checking in the drawers, in the little cupboard underneath. As he pulled one of the drawers out to get a better look, he sat down on the edge of the bed.

Something moved beneath him.

It was more than the springs, than the mattress shifting, there was something digging into him, a hard corner. He put the drawer back and got up off the bed, pulling the duvet back, the bedsheet, until the bare mattress was on display in front of him.

There was a rip down the centre of it, a tear that had been made with a knife that was already covered in blood. It had seeped into the white of the mattress, it had left drops, a mark where the knife had then been put down, you could see the outline of it in faint red.

And in the middle of the mattress was money, piles and piles of money.

"Zoe," Kidd said. She stopped her search, and joined him, standing next to him to look down at the pile of cash.

"Bloody hell," she breathed. "There's blood."

"Nina knew what she was looking for," Kidd said. "The mystery of the money is solved. She killed him, robbed him and then..."

"Someone got her back," Zoe breathed. "What do we do?"

"We didn't bring enough bags," Kidd said. "Get onto forensics. They're going to need to clear this whole place out."

———

THEY WAITED FOR THE TEAM TO ARRIVE, TAKING THEM through to the main bedroom, where they took pictures, took samples, and started to bag up all of the money. It took far longer than Kidd thought it would. There was so much of it. Even with the amount that Nina had taken, or even the amount that she had taken out with her to the club, there was still so much. For all they knew, there was still more of it in Nina's house. Maybe she thought this was a good idea. Maybe she'd stolen it and had been sleeping on a mattress full of cold, hard cash.

"She wasn't very careful," Kidd said as they made their way out of the house and back towards the station.

"What do you mean?" Zoe replied.

"She went in there, left her prints all over the place, and then just went upstairs and took that money," Kidd said. "She knew it was there, she went and took it and left a trail behind her. Once someone realised that Dwight was missing, or that he hadn't left the house in however many days, how long would it have taken us to figure out that Nina had killed him? If she were still alive, I mean."

"She'd stopped caring," Zoe said. "Maybe she figured her life was over either way. If she didn't kill him, he was going to kill her. If she got caught..."

Kidd couldn't fathom someone not caring about that happening to them. It didn't sit right in his head at all. But if she had been through hard times, if she had managed to pull herself out of those times before, maybe she thought she was untouchable. Or, like Zoe said, she didn't care anymore. It would just be over. Nina Hawkins wanted it to be over, one way or another. And she'd made sure it was.

"But who killed Nina?" Kidd asked. "That's what we need to know."

Zoe was about to answer when Kidd's phone rang in his pocket. He pulled it out, seeing that it was Powell calling from back at the station.

"What have you got for me?" Kidd asked.

"The Snake Pit has finally come through with their CCTV," Powell said.

"Thank Christ," Kidd said. "There was me thinking they were holding out on us because we shut them down. I was ready to go and knock some heads together. You started going through it yet?"

"Not just yet, sir, there's a lot of it," Powell said. "Just thought you might want to know."

"We're on our way back," Kidd said. "Start without us. We'll jump straight in when we get there." He hung up the phone and turned to Zoe. "Your boyfriend came through on the CCTV."

"Good for Seth."

"Good for Seth, good for Lawrence, good for us," Kidd said. "Let's go, can't have Powell having all the fun now, can we?"

CHAPTER
TWENTY-SEVEN

All eyes flew to Paige. She'd said it so simply, so matter-of-factly, like it was the easiest thing in the world. But she had just admitted to knowing about the murder of Dwight Griffith.

"You knew?" Janya asked, trying to keep the shock out of her voice.

"She told me she was going to do it," Paige said. "When things were getting bad, when he was threatening her and telling her that she needed to pay him back, she... She said she was thinking about taking matters into her own hands."

"Do you know when?"

Paige shook her head. "I didn't want her to tell me," she said. "I didn't want to believe that Nina was capable of something like that, but when she came home late one night last week, when I knew she'd not been working, and I knew she'd not been out on the town." She swallowed. "She wasn't wearing her shoes, her hands were... They were filthy. I wanted to believe it was mud, wanted to think she'd just fallen somewhere, but she..." She took a deep, shuddering breath. "She'd killed him."

"How did she—?"

"She stabbed him," Paige said. All of the blood seemed to drain from her face, like she might be about to pass out. She stepped towards the sofa, sitting on the edge of it, steadying herself. "She went to his house, they got into a shouting match, and she stabbed him over and over and over again until she knew that he was dead, until she knew that he couldn't hurt her anymore."

"She told you this?"

"She wasn't proud of it," Paige said quietly. "She wished that she hadn't done it. She said she couldn't get the feeling of the knife going into his flesh out of her mind. She couldn't shake the sound of him dying in front of her out of her head. It was drowning her. But at least she was free." She looked at the other girls. "She did it for herself, but she also did it for all of us. We're all free of Dwight now."

"Why didn't you tell anyone?" Janya asked.

"You expect me to report my friend to the police and tell them she's a murderer?" Paige asked. "He was threatening her life, it was her life or his. There was no other way it could have gone. Though I guess it doesn't matter now, Nina ended up dead anyway."

"But who killed her?" Bailey asked. There was a rising panic in her voice, like the severity of the situation had only just been made clear to her in the last few minutes. "I thought... I kind of guessed when you guys told me that she'd been killed, that it would have been Dwight that..." Bailey trailed off.

"You thought it was Dwight, but you didn't want to tell us because you wanted to save your own skin," Janya said, the disappointment laced into every word like a fine tapestry.

"It didn't matter in the end. He didn't do it, someone else did," Sienna said. "The question is, who?"

"Are we in trouble?" Bailey asked.

Janya wasn't wholly sure in what way she meant. Were the three of them in trouble for withholding information from the police? Paige might be in trouble for that. She'd known that Nina had killed Dwight, she had known that she was responsible for murder, and she'd chosen not to say anything. But maybe she meant it in the sense that there was a murderer still out there and they were connected to Nina, connected to Dwight. It was highly likely that all three of them were still in danger. But they had no leads—where to go next, who to speak to.

"Do you know of anyone else who was associated with Dwight Griffith?" Janya asked. "Was he the only one to give you money, or did he have associates? Did he have people that worked for him that you dealt with on different occasions?"

There was a chorus of nos in response, a cacophony of denial that Janya wasn't entirely sure she believed. She couldn't trust their word anymore, not after this. Though maybe she could still trust Paige. She'd told them about Dwight eventually, even if it had been somewhat under duress.

"Did you all take money from him?" Janya asked.

They all had. Every last one of them. Janya wasn't sure where to go from there. They'd hidden things from them, impeded their investigation, and now they had three bodies as part of this case, one of whom had been killed by another victim. Where were they supposed to turn next? Where were they supposed to go?

"I'm going to need you to talk me through what happened the night Nina died," Janya said. "And then I'm going to need to know where you all were the night before last, when Harper was killed." She took a breath and sat forward in her seat. "Leave nothing out. Sienna, we'll start with you."

IT TOOK FAR LONGER THAN JANYA WOULD HAVE LIKED, but they managed to get statements from each of the girls, alibis that they would be able to follow up on.

Anything else would be proven with the CCTV they were waiting on from The Snake Pit. It wasn't a good feeling to know that you'd been lied to, that you'd been deceived. It was an even worse feeling to know that Paige had stood there, finally telling the truth, and made both Sienna and Bailey realise the danger that they might be in despite Dwight's death.

"You okay?" Ash asked as they made their way outside and back towards the station. Truth be told, Janya was not okay. She didn't like that she felt like she'd been played by the girls; it just made her feel like there was even more that was being left out, that there were still parts of the story that were missing.

"Not really," she replied. "We're going to need to figure out what we want to do with Paige. She... She knew about the murder of Dwight Griffith."

"But she had no active part in it," Ash said. "She didn't help her hide a weapon, or conspire to kill him."

"But she didn't make it sound like she discouraged it either," Janya said. "She said it pretty plainly to the other girls. Nina did them all a favour by killing Dwight. She got him out of the picture and, in theory, saved them all."

"Except now there's someone else out there, taking these girls out one by one."

"Possibly," Janya said. "It might all stop with Harper."

"But you don't believe that, do you?" Ash asked.

"No," she replied. "I don't believe that one little bit."

CHAPTER
TWENTY-EIGHT

Powell wasn't joking when he'd said there was a lot of footage to go through from The Snake Pit. They trawled through it, frame by frame, trying to track down where exactly Nina was. At some point during their search, Janya and Ash returned and filled them in on their conversations with Nina's housemates. It was a good opportunity to take a break from staring at screens and fill everyone in on what had been going on. DC Hale and Powell made a quick trip to the kitchen and brought them all back coffee before they got down to it, Janya and Ash telling their tales first.

"She just came out with it?" Powell asked. Taking a sip of his coffee, he winced at it.

"Yeah, she knew," Janya said, turning her focus squarely on Kidd. "And I'm not sure what you want to do about that, boss. I mean, she wasn't necessarily involved in the murder, but she also didn't tell us about it. She knew. Is that perverting the course of justice? I don't know. She told us when it came out, she just wasn't upfront about it."

"I'll talk to Weaver about it, see what he wants done," Kidd said. "It confirms it, though, doesn't it? We've got the DNA, her prints, and now we have someone admitting that Nina was responsible for it."

"What did you find?" Ash asked.

Kidd told them about going to Dwight's house, about checking through notebooks and finding handwriting that looked exactly like his.

"Closing that loop," Ash said. "Nice."

"And then we stumbled on what had to be tens of thousands of pounds in cash stuffed into his mattress," Kidd said. A silence fell over the rest of the team. They were as shocked at the revelation as he had been to find it, it seemed. "It had been ripped open with a knife, it looked like. And there it all was."

"So you think—?"

"Nina stole the money after she killed him," Kidd said. "We know she was desperate for the cash. Maybe that's why she took it, maybe she took it as one last 'fuck you' to Dwight for all those threats. Those notes don't exactly make for comforting reading."

Janya chuckled. "So her last bit of revenge after stabbing him to death was robbing a dead man." She nodded. "Well, you've got to give it to her, she didn't do things by halves."

"But the question remains," Ash said. "If Dwight didn't kill Nina, then who did?"

"And how does it all connect?" Kidd added. They finished their coffees, Kidd taking a bit of time to go and speak to DCI Weaver about what they'd found so far, in the hope that it would postpone the press conference.

"Things seem to be getting more complicated, boss," Kidd said. "I don't know if us talking to the press is a good idea. It might just muddy the waters."

Weaver couldn't help but smirk. "You'll do anything to get out of talking to those vultures, won't you?" he said. "Fine, we'll push it back, but Superintendent Charles—"

"I'm begging you not to finish that sentence," Kidd said. "Thank you, boss."

Back in the Incident Room, they continued trawling through the CCTV, video after video. They were following Nina across multiple cameras, watching where she had gone. At one point, she was dancing with her friends, at another point, she'd gone to the bathroom, then to the smoking area, clutching her purse tight. That was one thing that they could all see her doing in every single frame.

She wasn't letting go of the purse, and she was paying for absolutely everything in cash.

"Got it!" Powell barked from one side of the room. "Did I win? Do I get a prize?"

"Shut up, Powell," Janya snapped.

"Said the loser."

"You're both children," Kidd grumbled as he made his way over to Powell's desk. Slowly, the team gathered around him, watching the footage over his shoulder.

Nina was standing at the bar. She was talking to someone. It might have been Paige, Kidd couldn't quite make it out. A figure sidled up next to her, dressed head to toe in black, a hood pulled close over their head.

Nina must have noticed because she held her purse a little bit tighter to herself before she moved it to the other side of her body.

They watched as the figure shifted where they were standing. A hand reached out, gloved, moving steadily towards the drink that was right behind Nina, just out of sight. She wouldn't have even noticed that something was dropped in her drink, wouldn't have even noticed the slight movement in the glass.

And the figure moved away, heading out of frame.

"Fuck's sake," Kidd grumbled. "Rewind it. Can we get anything from this?"

Powell went back, pressed play again. They all watched as something was slipped into Nina's drink, as the figure turned, pretty much still cloaked in shadow, and moved out of frame.

"Not a fucking thing," Kidd said.

"Aha, so Powell doesn't win," Janya said, moving back to her desk.

"No, he doesn't win," Kidd replied. "But we have a timestamp now. That was at 23:17. Let's find the footage from behind the bar, or from after that, see if we can't get her leaving." Kidd looked back at the evidence board. "And I want eyes on Blake Glover. Did you have any luck with him yesterday, Sanchez?"

"No, he wasn't at work."

"Fuck's sake," Kidd growled. "We need to talk to him. Nina's friends saw them fighting. We have to talk to him."

They kept going, kept searching. The footage from behind the bar was just as grainy, just as useless, except for confirming that whoever they were looking for was likely Caucasian. That was the best they could do. There was a flash of wrist as they put the drugs into Nina's drink.

"I've got Nina stumbling out of the bar," Zoe said a little while later. "The purse is gone."

"What?"

"The purse is gone," Zoe repeated. "I can't see where it went. Where did Seth say he found it?"

"Cloakroom," Kidd said. "She must have left it

somewhere when the Rohypnol kicked in, and then some Good Samaritan put it in the cloakroom, or gave it to the lost and found."

"If they'd opened it, they would have ended up with a pretty good night," Ash said.

"And a pretty guilty conscience," Janya added.

Kidd and the team watched as Nina stumbled out of the club at around 00:14, almost a full hour later. At what point had she lost her purse? Where had their hooded assailant been waiting? Had they been in the club still? Had they been waiting outside? They needed the footage from the riverside, from the restaurants down there. That would help, that would shed some light on this.

"We've got a timestamp, then," Powell said. "I'll get on to the restaurants, get them to send over whatever they have, see if we can't get something of her going down to the riverside."

"Sounds like a plan," Kidd said. The footage hadn't offered them much, just a timeline, a figure they could perhaps follow out into the night. "See if you can find that hooded person leaving the premises," Kidd added. "Better yet, see if you can trace them backwards through the club. That might help us figure out who it is."

"Good shout," Powell said. "Can you send that over to me, Sanchez?"

"Sure thing," she replied.

Kidd was about to leave Sanchez to do that when

he saw a figure get to their feet in the background of the video of Nina walking out of the club.

"Hang on," Kidd said. "Pause it."

Sanchez did as she was told, pausing the video. And Kidd could hardly believe his eyes.

Craig.

CHAPTER
TWENTY-NINE

"You've got to talk to him." They were the first words that Sanchez said to him when they walked out of the Incident Room to go and get coffee for the team.

Janya had started reaching out to the restaurants on the riverfront. Powell was tracing their assailant's movements through the club, hoping they could figure out who it was, where'd they come from.

He'd made screenshots too. You could just about make out the end of a nose in some of the bar footage. Maybe someone who had been in the club would remember this person, skulking around while everyone else was having a good time. They needed a bit of luck. They needed someone to recognise something about this person and come forward.

"I know," Kidd said. "I just... I told John last night."

"And?"

"And he didn't take it all that well," Kidd replied. "He wasn't angry or anything like that. He just left."

"He left?"

"He went home," Kidd said. "Shouldn't be reading into that quite so much, he does have his own flat after all, but it just felt... pointed."

"Well, he's bound to be upset, Kidd," Zoe said. "You've been holding a candle for Craig for goodness knows how long, and you always drop everything when he's around and do whatever you can to help him. That's bound to make him feel a bit insecure."

"But I told him he has nothing to worry about."

"Which is exactly what you say to someone when they have something to worry about," Zoe said. "I wouldn't overthink it, though that doesn't seem like your style. Just give him time. He'll come around. But you do need to talk to Craig."

"I know," Kidd said. "He didn't tell me he was there the night Nina died, which means there's a reason he kept it from me."

"Not necessarily," Zoe said. "But it certainly doesn't look good."

"Fuck's sake," Kidd said. "Whenever he comes back, trouble always follows."

"The common denominator is you, Kidd, I hate to say it," Zoe replied. "You're a magnet for it."

"Thanks, Zoe, I appreciate that," Kidd replied. "I just wish he'd come to me to talk about it. It's possible he hasn't because there's nothing to say, but... it doesn't look good."

"Agreed."

There was a knock on the door to the little kitchen area, DC Hale poking his head around the door. He looked nervous, like he didn't want to interrupt whatever discussion the two of them were having. Kidd wondered how much he had heard, how long he had been standing there before he had the confidence to knock and interrupt them.

"Sorry to disturb you," he said. "But I just got a call from Diane at the front desk."

"Already making inroads with Diane," Kidd said. "I'm impressed. If she likes you, you'll go far."

Ash laughed, looking a little sheepish all of a sudden. Perhaps Diane had already been turning on the charm. DC Hale was handsome and young; just her type.

"What can I do for you, Ash?" Kidd asked.

"Oh yeah, Diane called," he said. "There's someone to talk to you at the front reception. She said it was urgent."

Kidd and Sanchez made their way to the reception area, where they found that Diane wasn't in her usual spot behind the desk. She was sitting next to a girl, her arm around her, a box of tissues in her hand.

"It's going to be alright," she said quietly. "We'll get it sorted. There's no need to cry."

"Diane," Kidd said tentatively.

She looked up, and so did the girl. Kidd didn't recognise her straight away, but there was something about her face that seemed familiar. She was on their evidence board.

Bailey McBride.

"Oh, good," Diane said before turning her attention once more to Bailey. "DI Kidd and DS Sanchez are here. They'll be able to make sure you're alright, nothing to worry about at all."

She got to her feet, Bailey following suit, and Kidd got a proper look at her. Her eyes were red, her hair wild about her head like she'd not brushed it that morning. She was shaking, shaking wildly, like Diane had been the only thing to stop her from vibrating right off the chair.

"Bailey, what's happened?" Kidd asked. "Is everything okay?"

It was a stupid question. Clearly, there was nothing okay about the way that Bailey was feeling, but he needed the details. She didn't say anything, she just reached into her bag and pulled out a stack of cash. Twenty-pound notes bundled together with pieces of string.

As Kidd saw it, he felt the blood drain from his face.

"Come with us," he said, taking her further into the station.

CHAPTER
THIRTY

"How long have you had this?" Kidd asked. "Why didn't you give it to the officers who were at your property earlier today?"

Bailey looked so small sitting in front of them. She knew that she was in trouble, and with every passing second, she seemed to be getting smaller and smaller.

"I... I borrowed this from Dwight Griffith," she said. "It's the last of what I had. I... I thought... I don't know what I thought. But it's in the house and I think so long as it's in the house I am in danger and I need your help I can't... I can't... I don't want to die, Detective."

She was about to shatter into a thousand pieces before their very eyes. But she'd come here to speak to them. There was every possibility that meant she would be willing to give them information, or at least to give them something. Janya had been so certain that they were all hiding things. Maybe this was their opportunity to unpick all of that.

"Can you help me?" Bailey asked. "Can you protect me from... From whoever is doing this? Please?"

"We can do our best," Kidd said. "But if we're going to do that, we need you to tell us exactly what's been going on with the four of you," Kidd continued. "We have been getting the stories in dribs and drabs, but we need to hear the whole truth and nothing but the truth, do you understand?"

"Of course."

She started to cry again, great big sobs were racking her body. Zoe sat beside her, putting an arm around her, trying to help her calm down. She offered her tea, which Kidd gladly went and got for her. By the time he was back, Zoe had managed to get her to stop crying. She was breathing deeply, and Kidd knew that she was on the edge of another breakdown and didn't want to push her too hard.

"I wasn't here when it happened," Bailey said. "I was at home, but when I heard, when Paige told me, I knew I had to come back. I couldn't leave the girls to deal with it and..." She was desperately trying to pull air into her lungs, trying to stop herself from falling apart once again. "And I knew the money was in the house. I don't know about the other girls, I know that they borrowed from Dwight in the past, but they weren't getting threats from him, so I assume they paid him back. Or maybe they didn't, I don't know, but I didn't want to leave that money in the house and potentially be the reason that one of them was killed. I just couldn't take that."

"So that's why you're here?" Kidd asked. "You wanted to protect them?"

"Yes."

"Then why didn't you say anything when DC Ravel and DC Hale were at your house?"

"Because they were talking to us all together," Bailey said. "I didn't want them to know they were in danger, or that I was putting them in danger. I thought... I thought this would be the best way to do things, hand over the evidence and then... Then it's done, right? I'll be safe."

"What else do you know?" Kidd asked. "The only way we can help you is if you tell us the truth, everything."

Bailey took a breath, and it shuddered out of her. She was on the verge of absolutely falling apart. It was a difficult thing to watch, even more difficult when Kidd could only guarantee so much as far as protecting her went.

"It was Nina who found Dwight in the first place," Bailey said. "She was struggling the most out of all of us; I think that much was pretty clear. I think the girls have said as much, but she was the one who tracked him down and started borrowing off him.

And we saw how good things were for her, how much things had improved."

"Improved?"

"Well, she'd gone from freaking out about money on a near daily basis to... living quite well," she said. "She was buying nice food, new clothes, going out more, always being the one to buy the drinks. So we all, sort of, got involved."

"How?"

"She introduced us," Bailey said. "And Dwight came to us, or we'd go to him and we'd get money off him, he'd lend us some cash in hand or he'd bank transfer it. And he never really asked for it back, at least not right away. He had it to spare. He wanted us to be happy and comfortable until we were in a position where we could pay it back."

"And were you?"

"Yes," Bailey said. "Apart from this, I paid him back everything that he gave me."

"And the other girls?"

"Exactly the same as far as I know," Bailey said. "This was from two weeks ago. It was the last time I saw him. He gave me this and told me to tell Nina that he'd said hello."

"And did you?"

"I did," Bailey said. "And it sent her into an absolute spiral. She started asking me what he'd said, how he'd said it, was there anything else. And that's when I found out that he'd cut her off, that he wasn't going to give her money anymore because she wasn't paying him back and that he'd been threatening her for the last few weeks."

"How long?"

"The threats started about six weeks ago," Bailey said. "She showed me the notes, and I told her to go to the police, but she didn't want to. She had been to her parents, and they'd not helped her. She didn't think your lot would be of any use, so she said she was going to deal with it."

Kidd's blood ran cold at the phrase 'deal with it.'

"And what did you think she meant by that?" Kidd asked.

"I don't know," she replied. "You're going to think I'm really naïve now, but I just thought she was going to find a way to get the money. I didn't think... I didn't think that she was going to go and kill him."

Kidd hesitated for a moment, he felt himself do it, and watched the implication cross Bailey's face.

"You don't believe me," she said. "You have to believe me! I didn't want her to go and kill him, I just... I didn't want anything to happen to me or her. I thought she was going to... I don't know. I thought she might've found a way to pay back the money. Maybe she'd got another job. You have to believe me."

"We believe you," Zoe said. "We do, please don't panic."

"What do you know about Harper Gwynn?" Kidd asked.

"What?"

"DC Ravel said that none of your friends mentioned Harper Gwynn during their initial conversations," Kidd said. "Do you have anything to say about her? Or any insight there?"

"I was friends with her," Bailey said. "The other girls weren't so keen on her, I don't think, because she tried too hard."

"How do you mean?"

"She wanted the five of us to be friends, really wanted to integrate herself into the group, and I think that rubbed Paige and Sienna up the wrong way," Bailey said. "They were happy with us as a foursome, so they were rotten to her, kept calling her psycho behind her back, kept making it seem like her being worried about Nina when things were happening was a bad thing. But... I thought she was sweet. The three of us used to hang out together and..." She took her gaze away from Kidd, moving it to the coffee table in front of her, to the untouched cup of tea. "Because the three of us used to hang out, because I have connections with both of them, that's what has me thinking that maybe I am in trouble here. I don't... I don't want to be the next body on the borough. You have to help me."

Kidd waited while she took a sip of her tea, while she steadied herself once again. It had probably taken a lot for Bailey to come here today, to go against the friends whose thumb she seemed to be under. Janya hadn't been joking when she said Sienna ruled the roost, but Paige apparently wasn't much better.

"We'll keep you safe," Kidd said. "Sanchez will stay with you for the time being, and won't let you go home alone. We'll have some officers watching the property. Maybe it's best that you stay home for a bit, all three of you sticking together seems like a pretty good idea to me."

"Thank you," Bailey said. "I... I don't want to be a bother. I just didn't know where to turn."

"It's okay," Kidd said. "You did the right thing." He locked eyes with Zoe. "I just have to make a phone call."

Kidd walked out of the meeting room, pulling his phone out of his pocket. He dialled a number he'd not dialled for a very long time. They answered on the second ring.

"I wondered when I'd be hearing from you again."

"I need you to meet me," Kidd said. "Now."

CHAPTER
THIRTY-ONE

K idd made his way into town, waiting in Market Square for Craig. How much time had he spent over the years waiting for Craig? And here he was again, but this time, he needed answers.

He saw Craig before Craig saw him. He looked well, fresh, like he was actually managing to sleep while all of this was going on. When he caught Kidd's eye, he smiled, and Kidd felt a jolt go through him, a memory of how things used to be. When he'd wait for Craig after they'd both finished work; when they'd go somewhere for dinner or drinks; when their lives were completely intertwined, rather than two ships barely passing in the night.

"Morning," Craig said before checking his watch. "Yes, morning, just about. What can I do for you? You sounded very serious on the phone."

"I always sound serious," Kidd replied.

"Alright, Batman," Craig replied. "You want to go somewhere and get coffee so we're not out in the cold?"

"Cold is fine," Kidd said. "Let's go find somewhere a little more private."

They made their way out of Market Square, back towards The Bentall Centre, Kidd making the turn to take them into the churchyard. It was usually filled with homeless people, or day-drinkers getting their fix, but right then there were just pigeons on the grass, trying to find scraps. They flew up and into the cloudy grey sky as Kidd and Craig walked inside.

"How ominous," Craig said. He was trying to fill the silence. There was some comfort in the fact that Craig didn't seem to have any idea why Kidd had wanted to see him. He didn't have time to prepare answers or find ways to wrong-foot him.

They sat on a bench, Kidd turning his body to face Craig. Craig was sitting practically on the other end, almost like he couldn't bring himself to be close to Kidd. At least he knew he was in trouble.

"So," Craig started, still desperate to fill the silence. "What can I do for you?"

"You can start by telling me why you were at The Snake Pit the night Nina Hawkins was killed," Kidd said, locking eyes with Craig, holding firm. He wasn't about to let him dance around this. He needed answers, and he needed them now.

"I was there for a drink, a little dance," Craig said.

"I wasn't about to go to one of Andrea's pubs or clubs, I don't have a bloody death wish, Ben."

"Well, you're here," Kidd said. "That feels like enough of a death wish."

"So it's a crime for me to go and have a little dance, is it?"

"Don't bullshit me, Craig," Kidd snapped. "We talked yesterday, and you're telling me at no point did you think it was appropriate to tell me you were there the night that she died?"

"I didn't want to muddy the waters."

"Consider them fucking filthy," Kidd said. "What were you doing there?"

"I told you," Craig said. "I was having a drink, trying to find a way to escape from all the bullshit in my head, and the best way I could think of doing that was loud music and lots of alcohol. Why wouldn't I be there?"

"Did you see her drink getting spiked?" Kidd asked.

Craig blinked, shocked. "No."

"Craig."

"Ben," he said firmly. "Are you trying to tell me that you think I killed Nina Hawkins?" There was a softness to the way he said it, a way his voice had gone all musical, lilting, that immediately made Kidd stop believing anything coming out of his mouth. It was like he was putting on a performance, and Kidd wasn't there to be played.

"I'm trying to find out what it is you know and what the hell you're doing here."

"You want to know what I know?" Craig asked. He lowered his voice. "Are you sure?"

"Why are you asking me that?"

"Because it's a door that once opened can't be closed," Craig said.

"Go on," Kidd said.

"Andrea owns most of the places in Kingston, one way or another," Craig said bluntly. "Whatever way you slice it, she has this place mapped out. From The Queens Arms to The Hollow Tree to The Ram and beyond, if you dig around and look through all of the details, you can trace it all back to her. Shell companies upon shell companies, but she is there, she owns it." He paused, and Kidd thought it might have been for dramatic effect. "The Snake Pit is one of the few places that she doesn't have her claws in, and one of the few places one can meet a friend who is helping them tie up their loose ends."

"She owns that much of it?"

"She's got a little empire going," Craig replied. "You probably already knew that, but I'm just giving you a few more details because... well... it's pretty far-reaching. Maybe further than even you thought."

"So, who were you meeting?"

"I'm not about to answer that question," Craig said. "You even talking to me is getting you in heaps of trouble, I'm not about to add to the bloody pile, that will just make things all the worse."

"Craig."

"You don't want to know," Craig insisted.

"I want to know that you're being safe," Kidd said. "And I want to know that you're not... That you're not going to end up in the kind of trouble that means I'm investigating your death one day."

Craig seemed to soften at that, eyes looking a little glazed. They had a history together, and even though they weren't together anymore, they still cared for one another. After everything that they had been through, there was a tether that tied the two of them together, and that was not a tether that was easy to break.

Craig sighed. "People owe me money from within Andrea's company," he said. "I was meeting with a friend who was able to get me some of that money. He was taking it straight from Andrea's pocket and putting it into mine. It's just what I'm owed."

"And you're trying to tell me that doesn't put you in danger?"

"No," Craig said with a smirk. "I'm looking over my shoulder with every single step I take here, but I need that money. And I figured I had nothing to lose. I've already had to pick up my whole life and disappear once. If I get what I'm owed, I can disappear again, and then she won't ever see me again. This is the last of Craig Peyton."

"So that's it?" Kidd asked.

"Yes," Craig said. "Those are my loose ends. You already know too much. This is already putting you in danger, and I want to keep you out of it. If I can help it."

"You being here is putting me in danger," Kidd mumbled, sitting back against the bench. He stared out at the patch of grass. The pigeons had come back, gathering amongst the mud and dirt to try and find any scraps that they could. "I don't want you to get hurt."

"That's none of your concern," Craig said. "I'm here to tie up my loose ends, and then I'll be on my way. You won't have to see or think about me ever again."

Kidd looked over at him. "We both know that's not true," he replied. He took a breath, keeping his eyes locked on Craig's. "I need you to look me in the eye and tell me that you had nothing to do with the death of Nina Hawkins."

Craig looked him dead in the eyes, not blinking, not daring to. "I had nothing to do with the death of Nina Hawkins."

Kidd believed him. Kidd believed that he was here to tie up those loose ends that he was talking about, but until he was gone, he would be keeping his eye on the horizon, just in case Craig was there. Was his eye ever off it? Wasn't he always looking for him? Wouldn't he always be looking for him? Probably.

"So you had nothing to do with it," Kidd said. "But you were there, Craig. Did you see anything?"

"Like what?"

"We have CCTV of someone in dark clothes, hooded, head to toe in black," Kidd said. "They would surely have stuck out. Did you see them?"

Craig thought about it for a moment and Kidd wanted this last moment with Craig, if it were to be his last moment, to be one that he could spin into something positive. Let the lasting memory be Craig helping him figure this out and not coming back just to cause more trouble, to cause him more pain.

"When I got there, it wasn't all that busy," Craig said. "There was someone sitting in one of the booths dressed in black. I couldn't quite make out their face. The only reason I noticed them is because they were being asked to move by one of the servers."

"Asked to move?"

"The booths are VIP," he said. "So they get booked out, and the party had arrived and they had to go. They didn't make a fuss, they just went and found another place to stand. They weren't drinking, weren't doing anything really. Basically, they were doing a horrible job of blending in."

"You didn't see a face? No recognisable features?"

Craig shook his head. "My friend arrived, and I

lost sight of them," he said. "I think I saw them leaving later on in the night, but I didn't think anything of it. I think I was mostly surprised that they were still there. They must have been sweltering. It was hot in there, way too hot to be wearing all that gear."

"They were only wearing it to hide themselves from the CCTV," Kidd said, thinking that somewhere amongst all that footage there had to be a moment where they slipped up. There had to be something that would show their face. Anything at all. "Thank you."

"What for?"

"For being honest with me," Kidd said. "I hope you find what you're looking for."

"Thank you."

"I have to get back to the station," Kidd said, getting to his feet and pulling his jacket tightly around himself.

"Be careful," Craig said.

Kidd looked back at him. Craig hadn't moved.

"You too," he replied.

CHAPTER
THIRTY-TWO

Kidd couldn't shake that hollow feeling in his chest as he made his way back to the station. He walked by the river and looked out across the water, at the place where Nina had been found, trying to figure out if he'd missed anything, if there was something they'd not seen, that they'd not done.

There was movement to his right, a group of people smoking by the river, one or two of them vaping, the scent of tobacco mixed with the sticky sweet of whatever flavour they happened to be inhaling, clouding his lungs and making him cough. They nodded at him. He nodded back. He turned and walked back towards the station. Nothing felt safe anymore. Not a damn thing.

He was tempted to go to The Queens Arms and talk to Andrea, to confront her, to find out if she had anything to do with all of this, but that felt stupid, that felt like putting himself in harm's way for no bloody good reason.

Sanchez was waiting for him in the reception area when he returned, apparently deep in conversation with Diane. When she saw him crossing the road, she excused herself and stepped outside, joining him in front of the station.

"What happened?" She asked.

"Is Bailey okay?" Kidd asked. That felt like the most important thing at that moment.

"She's going to be," Zoe said. "We've sent her home with officers in tow. Weaver has made sure there will be uniforms watching their house from now until this case is closed. He said it was a smart call."

"Good."

"What happened?" she asked again, eyes fixed on him.

"Craig had nothing to do with it," Kidd said. "Or so he says. And Andrea isn't anywhere near that place. The Snake Pit is fully free of her grasp. Apparently, it's one of the last places in Kingston that is."

"You're joking."

"Apparently not," Kidd said. "If we trace ownership back of The Queens Arms, The Hollow Tree, The Ram, we'll find that they all belong to her. Shell companies on shell companies, he said. For all we know, The Druids Head is one of hers, and we've been drinking at an establishment owned by the bloody Kingston Mob."

"Well, that's a comforting thought, at least, isn't it?" Zoe said. "That she has nothing to do with The Snake Pit, so maybe that means she has nothing to do with this after all. There are no drugs involved, apart from the one put in Nina's drink, and I think we agree that she wasn't spending her time running Rohypnol around Kingston. So maybe this one isn't on her, and we can cross her off the list."

"But if it's not her, then who is it?" Kidd asked.

"Now, isn't that the question of the day?"

They made their way back into the station, the rest of the team waiting for them in the Incident Room. They were all waiting, all twiddling thumbs, and Kidd had that knock on the door that he'd been dreading.

Weaver stepped inside, a grave look on his face. "We've got the press gathering in the conference room now," he said. "It's go time, Kidd, make it happen."

"I thought you were postponing it?" Kidd asked. "I need more time, we've not got—"

"Kidd, the Super wants this happen and he wants it to happen now," Weaver said. "The press are at our heels. We just need to hold them off for a little while longer. You answer some questions, you make us look like we're doing our jobs as best we can, we move on."

"We are doing our jobs as best we can."

"I know that," Weaver growled. "Now, you just need to let them know that."

Kidd tried to think up a reason for it to be someone else, someone that wasn't him, but nothing came quickly enough.

"Kidd, I'm not waiting any longer. We have to do this. Now."

Powell slammed the receiver of his desk phone down so hard that Kidd jumped. Weaver practically leapt into the air as he turned around to face Powell, eyes blazing.

"What?" Weaver said. "Jesus Christ, what? Powell, you almost gave me a fucking heart attack."

"Blake Glover," he said. "Blake Glover came into work this afternoon. I've just had confirmation from the manager of Perkins. She said she wanted to let you know as soon as possible because she knows you want to talk to him."

"Get officers down there now," Kidd barked. "I want him interviewed as soon as humanly possible. If we can't get him quick access to legal representation, I'm going to flip my lid."

"Kidd, press," Weaver said.

"I know, I know," Kidd said, turning his attention to Sanchez. "Take the interview when he gets here. I want an iron-clad alibi, I want his prints, I want everything possible from this guy because if it's not him, I swear to God I'm going to lose it."

CHAPTER
THIRTY-THREE

To say that Blake Glover looked panicked would be the understatement of the century. From the moment that DS Zoe Sanchez stepped into the interview room, he wouldn't even meet her eyes. He kept looking around, his leg bouncing so severely before they'd even started the interview that she had to tell him to calm down. It was jostling the table, her tea was on the verge of spilling everywhere.

"I need you to take a breath for me, Blake," Zoe said, keeping her voice low. "You're not in any trouble, we just need to speak to you."

"You sent police down to arrest me, of course I'm going to think I'm in trouble," he replied, his voice coming out high and squeaky. From the photo that they had of Blake Glover, this wasn't the kind of attitude that Zoe had been expecting. In the picture, he looked intimidating, a grim-looking face, a square jaw, a buzz cut, but the way he was right now, he was like a puppy that someone had just kicked, cowering in the corner, practically whimpering.

"We've been looking for you for a couple of days, Mr Glover," Zoe said. "You didn't leave us with much choice."

"I would have come in."

"Of course," Zoe replied. She didn't believe that, not for a second. But she was also starting to doubt that Blake Glover was the man they were looking for.

Zoe started the interview by introducing herself, DC Janya Ravel, Blake, and his legal representative, a woman by the name of Jennifer Sharp. She looked nothing of the sort, a soft, older woman with the kind of half-moon spectacles you'd expect to see on a librarian, not a lawyer.

"Thank you so much for coming in, Blake," Zoe said.

"Like I said, you didn't give me much of a choice," he said. "I got dragged off by one of your lot while I was on the shop floor. It wasn't very dignified."

"Well, as I said, we've been looking for you for a couple of days," Zoe started. "When you heard about Nina Hawkins' death, did you not think it would be a good idea to come in and maybe have a chat with us?"

"I've not been well," he replied. "I've barely left the house. I think I must have eaten something funny on the way home from the club the other night."

Zoe smiled. "Given that you've brought it up, let's turn our focus to the other night, shall we?" Zoe said. "Can you walk us through what happened two nights ago at The Snake Pit, Mr Glover?"

Blake blinked. Maybe he'd not realised how much information they had on him, that they knew he was at The Snake Pit, that they knew that he'd got himself into some kind of altercation with Nina, and later on that night she had wound up dead. The panic seemed to rise in him again, the knee bounce returning in full force.

"I didn't kill her," Blake sputtered. "I didn't... I didn't think you'd need to talk to me because I didn't have anything to do with her. Not really."

"She was your manager at Perkins?"

"She was."

"And you got into a bit of a fight with her on the night that she died, did you not?"

Blake opened his mouth to respond, but apparently thought better of it. He looked across at Jennifer, and she nodded at him to continue. She was unreadable. Did she know that he'd had a fight with Nina? Was that why she was telling him to continue? Or did she have no idea and was just keen to hear the story for herself?

"I... I liked her, alright?" he said. "I told her about

it at work, said that I liked her and said we should go for a drink sometime."

"And what did she say to that?"

"She turned me down," he said. "She said it was a conflict of interest, given that I'm one of her staff, and that she didn't have time for dates at the moment. Then I saw when I was out."

"And how did it make you feel when you saw her at the club?"

"I felt like I'd been betrayed," he said. "She didn't need to lie to me. She said she didn't want to go out. I would have respected that, instead she lied and then she'd gone on a night out with her friends."

"That was none of your concern, Blake."

"I know, I know," he said. "But I was with my mates and... and I don't know, I got a bit too big for my boots, didn't I? I thought... I thought that I deserved an explanation, and they said I did, so I went over to her."

"And what happened?"

"It was loud in there," he said. "I couldn't really hear what she was saying, she couldn't really hear me, so we were shouting. I think... I think it must have looked a lot worse than it is."

"What did she say to you?"

"She wanted me to leave her alone, wanted me to... to fuck off, basically," he said, before blinking and looking between his legal rep and Zoe. "Can I say that? Sorry, didn't mean to swear."

"If that's what she said, that's what she said," Zoe replied. "So you had a fight. What did you do with the rest of your night?"

"I hung out with the boys," he said. "We left early because Deano wasn't feeling it, said we could maybe just get a couple of beers and go back to ours. We live in Surbiton."

"And did you do that?"

"That had been the plan," he said. "But we stopped off and got some food on the way home, and then... well..." He shuffled about in his chair. "I got sick. I had the food and it came back up almost immediately, don't think it had been cooked right and then I was just in bed. Didn't go into work for the past couple of days. Couldn't bring myself to, honestly. I've barely eaten, barely slept. But then my manager said if I didn't come in, then I'd be disciplined, so I went in today and..." He gestured to Zoe and Janya. "Then your lot came along."

Zoe looked at Janya and then back at Blake. He seemed to be telling the truth as far as Zoe could tell, but she didn't exactly expect him to come right out and say that he'd followed Nina out of the club and strangled her to death.

"Blake, I'm going to need contact numbers for your friends," she said. "And I'm going to have to corroborate your story, your alibi. You didn't leave the house at all the day before yesterday?"

"No," he said. "I couldn't even get out of bed. I've been an absolute wreck."

"Okay," Zoe said. "Give us the contact details. We will get to checking those. We'd like to take some DNA swabs if that's okay with you too, just so we can count you out entirely."

"I didn't do it."

"Okay," Zoe said. "Then you've got nothing to worry about, eh?"

CHAPTER
THIRTY-FOUR

With the weight of the world apparently on his shoulders, Kidd made his way through the police station and straight into the conference room. There was no time for him to complain to Weaver, no time to reason with him, to try and weasel his way out of it. The eyes of the local and national media were on him, and he had no choice but to speak to them now.

He was nervous as he took his seat on the podium. The sea of faces before him, some he recognised, some he didn't, was setting him on edge. Joe Warrington was there. He could see him in the crowd, a smirk on his face. He wasn't going to let Kidd get off easy here, there was no chance.

"Thank you so much for joining us this afternoon," Kidd started. He could feel his heart humming in his chest. Why was it that no matter how many times he did this, it never got any easier? He looked out at the crowd and saw, standing at the back, a grave look on his withered face, was Detective Superintendent Charles.

Fuck's sake, Kidd thought. *Just when I thought it couldn't get any bloody worse.*

Kidd cleared his throat. "This goes without saying, but I'm going to say it anyway because I know what you lot are like." There was a ripple of laughter that ran through the crowd. At least there was still the smallest amount of good humour among them. "This is an ongoing investigation. There are only so many details I will be able to give you, so please, bear with us and maybe try and keep those questions that I'm sure you all have, to things that I can actually talk about."

Kidd pulled out a statement and started to read. "Three days ago, the body of Nina Hawkins was found on Kingston Riverside. She was last seen leaving The Snake Pit, a club, at fourteen minutes past midnight. She was attacked and strangled to death. Autopsy report tells us that her drink had been spiked. We have video evidence of that occurring and are seeking any and all information that the general public may have on the person in the video. Two nights ago, Harper Gwynn, the ex-girlfriend of Nina Hawkins, was found strangled to death in her apartment. We believe these two deaths are connected and are currently seeking any information from the general public, who live in the area around Hampton Wick Train Station, of any unusual activity that may have been seen there. We are yet to make any arrests and are currently following any and all leads to get this solved in a timely manner. I will now answer questions for a short time."

Kidd took a breath as he put down the piece of paper and waited for the onslaught to begin. There was a flurry of activity as hands went up. Some people didn't wait to be called on, shouting their questions at him, like their volume would be enough for Kidd to take notice. It did the opposite. He wasn't about to tolerate rudeness or people calling out. He felt like a teacher.

Joe Warrington had his hand up and was waiting patiently at the back.

And he will continue to wait, Kidd thought, instead pointing to a young woman at the front of the crowd.

"Melissa Shepherd, Kingston and Richmond Gazette," she said, offering him a quick, thin-lipped smile. She had been at the slightly more impromptu press conference he'd given a few days ago. She didn't seem nearly as happy to see him this time around. "Given that there were drugs found in Miss Hawkins' system, should the people of Kingston, the women in particular, be worried about the rise in date rape drugs on the borough?"

"I would always advise people to be careful on nights out," Kidd said. "There are people out there who are carrying these kinds of drugs around and using them to take advantage of people, especially young women. Always be vigilant."

"So it is unsafe?"

"I don't think things have changed on that front," Kidd said. "If you asked me that question last week, I would have said the same thing. There are dangerous people out there, and we all need to be careful. We are working as quickly as we can to find out who was responsible on this occasion and bring them to justice."

"It's been a couple of days, and you don't seem to be any further along than you were the other day," Melissa continued. "And you've got another dead body. I don't see how that is going to give the public much faith in your ability to solve it."

"I have a pretty decent track record for that," Kidd replied. "We are working as hard as we can and as quickly as possible to get this solved. Any other questions?"

"Joe Warrington, Warrington's Wonderings," he said proudly. Kidd saw a couple of the other journalists roll their eyes. He wished Joe could see it. It was rather amusing. "Given the state of this investigation, as my colleague from the gazette rightly pointed out, do you think it would be best if this were handed off to another detective?"

"Anyone with questions that pertain to the case and aren't being used for clickbait?"

"Kidd," Weaver growled from Kidd's side. It was a cheap shot at Joe, he hadn't needed to fire back. That probably wasn't his smartest move.

"We are looking for anyone with information to please come to us and help us in our search," Kidd said. "We have stills from the CCTV, and anyone who might have been at The Snake Pit three nights ago is welcome to come forward and let us know if they saw anything. Anything at all," Kidd added. "No piece of information is too small."

He looked out at the journalists waiting for him to open the floor again to further questions, but he was done. He didn't want to deal with this anymore. He'd said his piece, he was out of there.

"Thank you for your time," Kidd said. He was about to leave the podium when he felt a hand on his arm, Weaver holding him back. They waited as the journalists filed out, as they made their way back into the corridor and out into the world to write their think pieces about how he was no longer fit for the job. He couldn't wait to see what Joe's piece would be like. Little prick.

"Hardly what I'd call a success." Superintendent Charles had made his way to the front of the room. Kidd was still sitting, and he wanted to stand, his feet were itchy. If he could stand, he could walk away. If he was seated, Charles could tower over him and make him look like a total prick.

"Well, I did what I could with the information we have," Kidd said. "We're doing our best, boss."

"Are you?"

"Yes, sir," Kidd replied, trying to keep his temper under wraps. Joe had rattled him, and it was that journalist from the gazette who'd given him a little nudge in that direction. *Fuck's sake.* "Actually, I'd quite like to get back to it if you don't mind." Kidd got to his feet.

"Actually, I do mind," Charles said sharply. "You've been on this case for a number of days, and progress has been slow, glacial."

"Three days," Kidd said. "In fact, it's barely been three days. Why are you breathing down my neck about this?"

"Because three days and you have two new bodies, and nothing has happened to solve who killed them."

"We found out that Nina Hawkins killed Dwight Griffith, so it's hardly nothing, is it?"

"Be that as it may," Charles said. "You are not working quickly or efficiently enough, and I have people I'm trying to convince that things in Kingston are safe. You are doing me no favours."

"I'm not trying to do you favours, sir, I'm trying to solve a case."

"Try harder."

Kidd stared into the deep, black orbs of Superintendent Charles's eyes. He'd always had it in for him,

Kidd knew that pretty well, but now he'd found a reason to come down on him, and he was taking great pleasure in it. Kidd could see it in the slight quirk at the sides of his mouth, at the way his eyes were glinting all shark-like. He was pleased with himself.

Kidd looked at Weaver, still sitting down, not saying a word. He didn't have faith in Kidd anymore either, that much was clear. He'd lost that faith somewhere during this case. Maybe it was all Kidd's fault for losing focus, for focussing on Craig, on Andrea, instead of on what he should have been focussing on.

"I'm going to excuse myself," Kidd said, "and get back to my investigation." He looked at the two detectives. "Assuming it is still my case," he added sharply.

"It is," Charles said. "For now."

Kidd didn't say another word. He walked out of the conference room and into the cold night air to take a breath. He hated this feeling in the pit of his stomach, this feeling that he wasn't good enough, that he wasn't doing enough. He was doing all he could.

Then where do we go next? he thought, but he had no idea.

"How was it?" Zoe asked as Kidd went back into the Incident Room. The bollocking from Superintendent Charles had taken it out of him. The chat with Weaver afterwards wasn't enough to paper over that wound. He was hoping to come back to speak with Zoe and for her to tell him they'd charged Blake or something. It was a long shot.

"Awful," Kidd said. "Super decided it was the perfect moment to come down and watch me get absolutely skewered by the media. So that was fun. Weaver did fuck all to protect me from it, too. I think he thinks I've lost my knack."

"You've been doing your best."

"I've been distracted by Craig," Kidd said. "I kept turning to him or to Andrea and thinking that was where the heart of this case was, but I was wrong, the heart of this case is with Nina. It's with the people who have been killed, and I totally missed that." He took a breath. "How did it go with Blake?"

"He had an alibi for both nights," Zoe said. "He was really bloody sick apparently, says he's got a housemate who can vouch for it. He's not left his property. And he openly admitted to the fight with Nina, admitting that the way he behaved with her was unacceptable. He liked her a lot. I would have gone so far as to say that he loved her, but instead of being halfway normal about it, he decided to start getting at her about it any chance he could get."

"Sounds like a great guy," Kidd said. "He's not our man?"

"We're going to check on his alibis," Zoe said. "He's got mates who will be able to corroborate what time he headed home from the club and a house-mate who can tell us whether he actually got there, and a little bit of CCTV will go a long way. Powell is going to get on it first thing in the morning."

"And what about you?"

"I was waiting here to tell you that, and to make sure that you were doing okay after the press conference," she said. "I was actually going to see if you wanted to go for a drink, but I get the impression that after all this, you're going to want to go home and see John, smooth things over there."

"Yeah, I reckon that's probably my best bet," Kidd said. His phone rang on his desk. "Fucking hell, it never ends."

"Who is it?"

Kidd checked. "Unknown number," Kidd said.

"Answer it," Zoe replied.

Kidd didn't want to. The only person he could think of who would be calling him from an unknown number would be Craig, and he wasn't sure he wanted to hear any more from him. He wanted to forget that Craig was in town, to pretend like he didn't know what he already knew.

But what if he was in trouble? What if the loose

ends he was planning on tying up turned out to be harder to put together than he first thought?

"Kidd," Zoe snapped.

Kidd answered the phone. "Hello?"

"Bloody hell, you took your time," the voice on the end of the phone said. It was not the voice he'd been expecting. "I've been trying to call you for the last hour."

Andrea.

Andrea Peyton.

"Well, I've got a case to solve. I was in a press conference," Kidd said, leaning on his desk. "Anything I can help you with?"

"Plenty," she replied. "I'm waiting outside for you. Come alone, or you won't be going back at all."

She hung up, leaving Kidd staring at the handset.

"Who was it?" Zoe asked.

"Andrea," Kidd said. "She's outside."

"Kidd—"

"Don't."

"What do you mean 'don't'? You can't go out there," she said.

"She wants to talk," Kidd said. "What's the harm in talking to her?"

"You could end up in a body bag, that's what the harm is," Zoe said. "Talking to Craig was one thing, dancing with the devil is another."

"I'll tell her you said that," Kidd replied.

"I'm begging you not to go out there," Zoe said.

"It's dangerous. You know it's dangerous. You can't do this."

"She's not going to do anything to me outside the station," Kidd said, "She wouldn't be that stupid. She wants to talk. So we're going to talk." He took a moment. "She said to come alone. Please don't follow me."

Zoe went to protest, but thought better of it. She went back to her desk and sat down, turning her attention back to whatever was on her screen. She didn't like this, and she was making it very clear that she didn't like it. But Kidd knew what he needed to do.

Kidd made his way out of the station and into the frigid night. He looked around—across the road, down the street, trying to spot Andrea. And then a figure waved. She was waiting outside The Rose Theatre, sitting on a nearby wall, hands stuffed in her pockets.

Kidd went over to her. He was aware of the cameras that were around the place, the ones outside the theatre, outside the front of the police station. She wasn't about to do anything here, but he was more concerned that he would be standing there talking to someone who was currently under investigation. Neither one of them had the upper hand.

"It's Baltic," Andrea said. "Only time I can remember it being worse was when we were down on the coast."

"Are you trying to soften me up with fond memories?" Kidd asked. "I wouldn't bother."

"Alright then, I'll cut to the chase, shall I?" She took her hands out of her pockets, and Kidd felt himself tense, like she was about to uncover a weapon. Instead, she just moved her hair out of her face. "Someone is skittish."

"Someone else is stalling," Kidd said. "What do you want?"

"So impatient," she said, scrunching up her face at him. "And so rude about it too. I just wanted to talk."

"I find that hard to believe," Kidd replied. "Please, just tell me what you want from me so I can be on my way."

"Where is Craig?" she asked.

Kidd stopped, turned, and watched her carefully in the dark.

"That got your attention, didn't it?"

"What makes you think I know where he is?"

"He's back," she said. "My people have seen him skulking around. I want to know what he's doing here. I want to know where he is, so that I can have a conversation with him. It's been such a long time since I've seen my dear brother."

"The same dear brother that you forced to work for you and then tried to frame for murder," Kidd replied. "And then tried to track down so you could exact your revenge? Andrea, it's practically Shake-spearean, and he's hardly your *dear* brother."

"Where is he?"

"I don't know."

"Bullshit."

"No, Andrea, it's not," Kidd replied. "I know he's back, I've spoken to him, but you know Craig, he plays his cards pretty close to his chest and he has no interest in telling me what he's doing here and, frankly, I'm not sure I want to know."

"Because if you know, you'll want to help."

"Exactly," Kidd replied. "And I've got myself into enough scrapes for Craig Peyton in my time. So no, I don't know where he is. I'm keeping out of it."

She smiled, her mouth a thin line. "That's something I can get on board with."

"I'm sure," Kidd replied. "Goodbye, Andrea."

CHAPTER
THIRTY-FIVE

Kidd made his way back inside, DS Sanchez immediately collaring him in the hallway when he arrived. It was clear to him that she had been watching from the corridor, out of sight, or at the very least, out of sight of Andrea. If anything had happened to him, she would have been ready to pounce.

Kidd would never have asked her to do something like that, putting herself at risk for him, but he was grateful nonetheless. It was always good to know that despite all of his fucking about, she still had his back.

"What happened?" she asked. "It looked intense."

"You could see it from here?"

"I have very good eyesight," she said. "And you decided to stand right near some streetlights, which made it a little easier for me. What did she say?"

Kidd sighed. He was still processing it.

"She wanted to know where Craig was."

"Did you tell her?" Sanchez asked.

"Of course not," Kidd replied. "Well, actually, there was nothing to tell. I've been keeping my distance, remember? So I have no idea where he is or where he's staying. I barely know what he's here for. I don't want to know."

"Without sounding like a total dick here, I think that's for the best," she said. "Where he goes, trouble follows, and I think after what happened last time, you need to do your best to keep out of it."

"Agreed," Kidd replied. "I've not seen her in such a long time, just seeing her made me feel... cold. "

"I'm not surprised," Zoe said. "She's not the nicest of acquaintances. You going to be okay?"

"Yes," Kidd said, knowing full well that anyone who crossed Andrea was bound to end up in some kind of trouble. "I'm in the very fortunate position that this time around I'm not hiding anything from her. I have nothing to do with her whatsoever. I don't know where Craig is. I'll be fine."

"Are you sure?" Zoe asked.

Kidd thought about it for a moment, trying to push that sick feeling in his stomach down, down, down, as far as it would go.

"Not really," he replied. "But let's get ourselves out of here, shall we? Everyone else has gone home.

We might as well salvage something of an evening for ourselves."

They got themselves together and made their way out of the station. Seth was there to pick up Zoe, wanting to take her out for dinner and likely make sure she got home safely given everything that was going on.

Kidd said his goodbyes and started back through town and towards his house. It was a rare day that Kidd actually felt nervous while he was walking home. The fact that Andrea had been nearby, the fact that she had been watching, was setting him on edge. It likely meant nothing, but there was something in knowing that she was watching him that had him checking over his shoulder every few steps, that had him wondering if there was anyone waiting around corners for him.

When he reached the Old London Road, he saw Perkins on the corner. It was closed now, had likely been for the past couple of hours. That had been their last hope, their last chance. What could they do now? Where could they turn? They would have to wait and hope that someone would see the appeal, that someone would reach out to them with information that they could use to push the investigation forward.

Kidd started down the Old London Road, past the closed shops, the darkened windows, past The Hollow Tree with its music pumping out into the dark. He was a stone's throw from home, and he had no idea what would be waiting for him when he got there.

He'd barely thought about John all day, barely had a chance to, given everything that had been going on. He felt guilty that his partner had barely crossed his mind. He hadn't even messaged him. He didn't even know Kidd was on his way home.

He pulled out his phone, typing a message to John.

KIDD

Sorry for the radio silence today. Wondered if you were coming to mine. Would love to see you if—

Something hit the back of his head, knocking him to the ground. He hit the deck hard, wind knocked out of him, hands scraping on the pavement, knees crashing, crunching, shoulder injury suddenly back in full force. Jesus Christ, what had hit him?

He managed to roll over in time to see a figure dressed in head-to-toe black standing over him, glaring down. They threw another punch, and another, connecting with his face each time. Kidd could taste blood, he was seeing stars, he could barely fight back, he could barely move.

Then hands closed around his throat. He held on for dear life, wrapping his hands around the wrists of his assailant, trying to pull them off, but they were strong, or the wind had been knocked out of him so incredibly that he just couldn't find the strength to fight, to get away, to escape.

His vision started to tunnel, his world starting to fade to black.

The hands disengaged from around his throat. The weight on his chest released. A familiar voice called his name, as he scratched his way back out of the blackness, the tunnel receding.

Kidd's eyes focussed in time to see a figure dressed in black running away, their hood down, a flash of long, dark hair heading off into the distance. He looked up at his saviour. The man who had been there for him, who had stopped him from having the life squeezed out of him entirely.

"John," Kidd managed before the darkness took him, and he passed out.

CHAPTER
THIRTY-SIX

The world flickered into focus around Kidd. The room was spinning. Nothing was as it should have been. He tried to steady himself, tried to open his eyes some more, but the light hurt, his body hurt, his face hurt, everything hurt.

"Fucking hell," he groaned.

There was movement near him, a flash of black in his periphery. He moved a little too quickly, shifted himself in the bed and cried out. The pain was excruciating and seemed to run through his entire body, all the way to his face. He felt puffy, bruised, like someone had gone at his head with a hammer.

"Ben! Ben, what the fuck? Are you awake? Ben?"

John's voice. It was John. John, who had been there to get the person off him. John who had been there to look after him even after everything that had

269

happened, after all of the shit, after all of the Craig drama that just didn't seem to go away.

"John," Kidd said. "Fucking hell, John, what happened?"

"You were attacked, Ben. Stop trying to move, for fuck's sake," he said.

Kidd stopped moving, stopped trying to, he just focussed on trying to get the light to not hurt, to be able to open his eyes. John was sitting next to the bed. He must have slept in the spare room, if he slept at all.

Kidd looked a little closer. He didn't look like he'd slept. Had he been waiting up all night, watching over him? He turned his attention to the window. It was light out. What time was it? Was it the morning? The afternoon? He'd passed out. He remembered that part. John must have—

"How did you get me back?"

"I carried you," he said. "Well, it was more a drag than a carry; I'm not that strong."

"Rude."

"You're obviously feeling a little better if you're making jokes."

"Not too shabby," Kidd said. "Just feel like I've been hit by a bus."

"Not a bus, a person," John said. "Though I didn't see what happened, you might have to fill that part in for me. You were just..." He shook his head. "I wasn't even sure it was you, I was just... I was trying to protect whoever it was that was having the shit beaten out of them and then..."

Kidd had a dark thought. He couldn't stop it from crossing his mind.

"If you'd known it was me, would you still have helped?"

John reached forward and took Kidd's hand. "I would have run over even faster," he said. He gave Kidd's hand a squeeze. "Did you... Did you see who did it?"

Kidd thought about it. He tried to remember exactly what he'd seen. When he'd looked up at the person who had attacked him, all he could see was black. He was staring into nothing but black. But then they ran. John chased them away. There was a flash of dark hair. Nothing more, just a flash of something.

"I saw dark hair," he said. "That's... that's all." He swallowed. "What time is it?"

"Almost noon."

"And I'm still at home?"

"You're at Kingston Hospital," John said.

"I'm what?"

"I got you into the back of the car and I drove you to the hospital," John said. "You'd passed out, but once you came to, I was trying to keep you awake. I didn't know if you were concussed or—"

"I have to get to work."

"Ben!"

271

"What?"

"You can't go to work. You're in the hospital, you need to rest, are you out of your fucking mind?"

"Where's my phone?"

"It's on the bedside table," John said. "It's been buzzing off the hook all morning. I told Weaver you weren't coming in, that they needed to carry on without you. Apparently, the rest of your team hasn't got the message yet."

"I have to go in," Kidd said. "I have to go in. They have to know what I know."

"What do you know?"

"That whoever it was that tried to kill me is the person we are looking for in all of this," Kidd said. His voice was loud, louder than he intended it to be, and in the silence that followed his hearing seemed to come back into focus. He could hear the sound of footsteps outside on the ward, he could hear the movement of the curtain that was around half of his bed, hear the rustling of the sheets. He was in the hospital. Why was he in the hospital? The last place he needed to be was the hospital.

His phone started buzzing again. He could see POWELL across the front of it. He locked eyes with John.

"Ben, don't answer it," John said. "Let them deal with this themselves. You don't have to jump in and save the day."

"I'm not jumping in and saving the day," Kidd

said, unable to keep the bitterness out of his voice. "I'm doing my job." He picked up the phone. "Hello?"

"Are you okay?" Powell's voice sounded a little panicked. "I've been trying to call you for the past hour."

"Had a bit of a situation last night," Kidd said. "Little bit of trouble. Everything okay?"

"It's not really," he said. "Where are you?"

"Doesn't matter," Kidd said. "What's up? Why are you calling me?"

"Sienna is missing," Powell snapped.

"What?"

"She's missing and Paige is at the station completely fucking terrified," Powell said.

Kidd looked over at John. He knew he should stay where he was, knew he shouldn't be leaving the hospital, knew he shouldn't be carrying on with work like nothing had happened but...

"I'm on my way," he said.

He just couldn't help himself.

"I WANT YOU TO KNOW THAT I THINK YOU'RE A FUCKING idiot," John said as he drove Kidd away from Kingston Hospital and towards the station. It wasn't that far, just a straight shot through town, but John wanted to make sure he got there okay. It was the kind of sweetness and care that told Kidd that he shouldn't even be doing this, that he needed to have his fucking head examined. Literally.

"I know," Kidd said. "But I can't... I just can't let this go."

"I hate this so much," John said. "I swear you are taking years off my life."

"But what an adventure."

"Fuck off, Ben."

John pulled up in front of the station, looking over at Kidd. "I am begging you not to go in there. I am begging you to call Sanchez and let her know that she is taking over this case, that you need your rest."

Kidd swallowed. "I'm sorry, John, you know I can't do that," he said. "I have to see this through."

"Then I can't stop you," he said. "But for fuck's sake, you need to message me every hour on the hour and tell me that you are okay or I am going to come to this station and make such a bloody nuisance of myself."

"Good," Kidd said. "I'd like that."

He leaned over and gave John a quick kiss before he got out and made his way inside. His face was a fucking state. The two hits that his attacker had got in on him had left him looking like a total mess, and apparently it looked even worse than he thought, because Diane physically recoiled as he walked into the reception.

He made his way through to the Incident Room

where his team were waiting, Ash with his eyes glued to his screen, Janya on the phone, Zoe and Powell the only ones who looked up at him when he walked in.

"What the fuck happened to you?" Zoe asked.

"It's a long story," Kidd said. "I'll explain, and you can tell me what's happened to Paige."

"More than that, boss," Powell said. "Ash is onto something. We may have a few more details for you about our killer."

"Good stuff," Kidd said. "No time to waste. Let's get back to work."

CHAPTER
THIRTY-SEVEN

"I'm sorry, you have had the absolute shit kicked out of you and you decided to leave the hospital and come into work," Zoe said. "I feel like I should be sending you back for a bloody brain scan. What is wrong with you?"

"I saw them," Kidd said. "I'd had the shit kicked out of me by them, but I saw them. We are talking, long, dark hair, and who do we know out of this line-up who has long dark hair, who isn't Sienna?" Kidd made his way over to the Evidence Board and tapped on Bailey's picture.

"Bailey?" Zoe asked. "But she was here yesterday; she was in pieces."

"Exactly," Kidd said. "And she handed over some money, and told us how scared she was, all things she wouldn't do in front of her housemates."

"And then she followed you home and tried to finish you off too?"

"I've got the marks around my neck to prove it," Kidd said. "What's going on with Paige?"

"She's in a meeting room, she's got tea, she's got biscuits, she's got a lovely PC with her, Sasha Calvin, she's calming down," Zoe said. "We figured you'd want to have a chat with her. She's absolutely losing it."

"I'm not surprised," Kidd said, looking over at DC Hale. He was still staring at his screen, clicking away. Kidd was running out of patience. "What have you got, Ash?"

"I've got someone with dark hair and a pale face," Ash said. "Got it on the CCTV of them going into Harper's building and coming out about half an hour later. They made quick work of it." He clicked a few more times, turning the screen around and showing Kidd exactly what it was that he had. Kidd looked at them hard. There was something about them that didn't quite make sense.

He looked back at the evidence board and then back at the screen, his brain doing somersaults to try and figure out what on earth, or rather, who on earth, it was he was looking at.

"You're seeing this?" Kidd said.

"I am," Sanchez replied. "Problem?"

He swallowed. "Potentially," he said. "Can I talk to Paige? Is she available?"

"She is," Zoe said. "No time like the present. Let's keep this moving."

PAIGE SEEMED SHOCKED AT THE STATE OF KIDD, almost scared of how much of a wreck he looked in that moment. She didn't need to say anything, her face said it all.

"Your pal did this," Kidd said. "We'll thank her when we find her, shall we?"

Paige chuckled, a dark sort of chuckle that Kidd could almost tell she didn't really mean. It was hiding all the pain she was feeling. All the fear.

Kidd had a brief chat with PC Calvin before sending her on her way, thanking her for staying with Paige, for looking after her, before turning his attention squarely on Paige.

"Silly question, I know, but are you okay?" Kidd asked. "I imagine today has been a lot for you."

Paige breathed a shuddering breath. Her hands were shaking, and she kept them moving like she didn't quite know what to do with them.

"It's been awful," she said. "Just awful. We were supposed to stick together. We were going to look after one another, that's what this was, we were going to look after one another so none of us got... So we didn't..."

She took a deep breath, looking at the ceiling, trying to stop more tears from coming.

"You did the right thing coming to us," Kidd said. "We can look after you if you're here."

"I didn't know what else to do," Paige said. "I went to Sienna's room this morning, went to go and make sure she was okay. But she wasn't there. I tried to call her, tried to text her, I phoned her Mum, her sister, I did... I did everything I could think to do. She's gone. She's fucking gone. I don't know what I'm going to do." She started to cry, the tears rolling down her face, her hand flying to her mouth as she tried to silence herself. "You were supposed to stop this from happening. You were supposed to keep us all safe. You sent bloody police officers to watch the house and look what happened? It's still happened."

"I'm sorry," Kidd said. "The only thing I can do is apologise and ask if there is anything else you know that might be able to help us figure out where she has gone?"

"I... I don't know where they might have gone," Paige said, and Kidd felt himself deflate. "But..." And immediately he was on the edge of his seat again.

"We talked about... We talked about ways that we could look out for one another, things that we could do to make sure that... we could find each other."

Kidd waited for Paige to continue, for her to tell him what she was getting at.

She reached into her pocket and pulled out her

keys. There were all sorts of little keyrings and charms on them, little knickknacks from holidays, memories, a picture of the four of them together on a holiday somewhere that looked hot.

She rummaged through them and showed Kidd a little square-rimmed thing with pink piping. It didn't look like anything much, a trinket, a small something that might have had some writing on it at some point, some kind of print.

"What is this?" Kidd asked.

"It's a tracking device," Paige said.

Paige New was a genius in DI Kidd's eyes in that moment. It had been Sienna's idea in the first place. She had come to Paige and said that she was going to give her the tracking device that she had for her keys, and that Paige could do the same, and then they would be able to find one another if something happened, if the worst happened.

It was a beautiful idea, a beautiful way for them to still be able to look after one another, and right then, it might have been the only thing that helped them find Sienna.

Paige opened the app on her phone and showed Kidd where they were. It looked like... It couldn't be.

"What the fuck are they doing at The Snake Pit?" Kidd asked.

CHAPTER
THIRTY-EIGHT

Kidd wasted no time. He got in touch with Weaver, begging him to send backup to the closed club. He gathered the team, and they made their way into town. Any uniforms they'd managed to gather on short notice were coming with them, some to be stationed outside the front of the club, others to be stationed at the various fire exits around the perimeter. They couldn't take any chances here.

They made it to The Snake Pit in good time, Kidd leading the way as they walked up the stairs from the riverside and to the front door. The closed notice was still on the door, but he could see even from a distance that the door was open. It was only open a little way, just enough that you could maybe be forgiven for ignoring it if you didn't already know that there were people inside.

"Give me a head start," Kidd said. "They're not

going to be expecting anyone. We don't want to spook them, not straight away. Give me a few minutes."

"A few minutes?" Sanchez said. "Could you be a little more vague?"

"Three minutes," Kidd said. "Unless you happen to hear some kind of commotion, in which case, use your best judgment.

Kidd started inside, Sanchez, Powell, Ravel and Hale behind him, waiting by the door. There were lights on. The sickly-sweet stench that had been there before was nowhere to be found. It had been replaced with the smell of bleach, the stench of cleanliness.

They had obviously cleaned it before they had closed up, making sure the place would be somewhat presentable for when they came back. Given what was happening, Kidd wasn't so sure that would ever happen.

He stepped into the space, not totally sure what he was going to see when he got there.

The emptiness of it was what struck him first, the bleach in the air, hanging there, lingering where there was so little ventilation. And there, sitting at the bar, was Sienna. She was alone and, as far as Kidd could tell, entirely unharmed.

"What is going on?" Kidd said quietly to himself as he made his way inside. He was vulnerable in here, but they outnumbered whoever was responsible. So that was something.

"What... What are you doing here?" Sienna squeaked from the bar. She looked genuinely confused. Was she panicking? Kidd couldn't tell why she would be panicking. "You... You're not Paige."

There was movement to his right, and Kidd saw someone coming out of the dark. He saw the flash of black, the dark hair swinging wildly as someone came towards him at full force. He dodged out of the way, throwing himself across the floor and watching as the person steadied themselves in the space where he had been just a few moments before.

He kept his eyes on them as they moved in the darkened corner of the club, as they straightened up, as they stared him down from the dark.

He looked back over at Sienna, who was still sitting at the bar, sitting there like that hadn't just happened, like Kidd hadn't just nearly been attacked. Were they working together?

"Don't move!" Kidd barked. "You're trapped in here, we're all trapped in here, we have the entire place surrounded, there is no use fighting any of this. Bailey, just give yourself up. There is no point fighting it anymore."

"Bailey?" The voice in the dark said, mockingly almost. They stepped into the light, pulling their hood back and revealing a face that Kidd didn't recognise, at least not entirely. "I'm not Bailey," she said. "I'm Maggie. I'm Sienna's sister."

CHAPTER
THIRTY-NINE

It was the one person Kidd hadn't heard about during this entire case, someone that Janya had mentioned in passing after she had gone to see the girls a second time around to get more information. The sister who had come down to look after Sienna.

When he'd been at the station and seen the CCTV image from Ash, he knew that something hadn't been quite right. It wasn't the clearest shot of the face, but it was enough that he could see that his hunch about it being Bailey wasn't quite right. But he didn't know who else it could have been. He didn't know who it was he was looking for. Until now.

He stepped back from the pair of them, keeping them both in sight. Outside, he may have the numbers, but in here, he needed to keep them distracted for as long as possible. He was fairly sure he'd be able to overpower them in a fight, but in his current state, he was struggling to keep himself upright. Just one dive across the floor, and he was practically gasping for breath.

"Someone needs to start explaining," Kidd said. "There are officers outside. There is no way out of this for either of you. What is going on?"

Maggie seemed to relax a little at the very mention of there being officers outside, the tension in her shoulders vanishing, the life seeming to drain out of her. Maybe on some level, she wanted to get caught. Maybe she was almost glad that this was the end of whatever the hell it was she was trying to achieve with all of this.

Kidd had no idea. Kidd hadn't even spoken to the girl. He'd not spoken to Sienna either; all his information about her had come via DC Ravel. He suddenly realised how disconnected from this case he had been, how his focus hadn't been there, how he'd not had his head in the game as he'd done during previous cases. This shouldn't have happened. He should have known who this person was.

"I started it," Maggie said. "I... I need you to know that Sienna had nothing to do with this. She knew about it. I told her about it. I... I did it."

"What did you do?"

"I killed them," Maggie said. "I killed Nina and... and then I killed Harper. I was going to kill Paige, too, when she got here. I'd started it. I needed to finish it before... Before you got to the bottom of it all."

"Finish it?"

"Close the circle," Maggie said. "I needed to take out Paige. She was the last one. It felt... I don't know. It felt believable that Sienna would be okay. The final girl."

"The final girl?"

"Like a slasher film," Maggie said. She was so casual about it, so cavalier, like she didn't give a fuck at all about what had happened, about what it was that she'd done. Paige would have just been another body, another person to add to the list.

"What about Bailey?"

"In her room," Maggie said. "Last night. I got her. I made her a cup of tea before she went to bed, and I slipped a little something in it so she'd be totally out of it, and then I finished the job. Paige was the last one."

"Did she not look for Bailey this morning?"

"I told her she'd gone home," Sienna said. "She bought it. Didn't think anything of it. She believes pretty much anything I say, so it wasn't hard to convince her to have our locations. It meant we could lure her here, that we could finish the job, and... move on."

"Why?" Kidd asked. It didn't compute in his head. Why would they do something like this? What on earth did they stand to gain?

"It was Nina's fault," Maggie said, and there it was. Kidd could see the rage bubbling beneath the surface of Maggie Parks. "She was the one who started all of this."

"All of what?"

"The money borrowing," Maggie said. She looked over at Sienna and then back at Kidd. "It was Nina who got Sienna to do it, who told her it would be fine. She told her that everything would be okay if she just borrowed a little bit of money here and there. And sure, my sister was stupid. She took more than she could afford. She started spending like there was no tomorrow, but if Nina hadn't brought it to her—"

"And that was worth killing her?"

"She nearly ruined my sister's life," Maggie said. "That piece of shit Dwight Griffith took our family for everything they had. And I told Nina about it. I told her what she'd done, and she didn't take any responsibility for it."

Kidd looked at Sienna. "Is that true?"

"I took too much," she said. "I took too much money, and it was so much that I couldn't pay it back, and Dwight was getting on my case, and... I turned to Nina for help, and she wouldn't help me, wouldn't talk to him for me, said she had her own things to settle with him. It was my family who bailed me out. My parents, Maggie... They gave up everything for me."

"And then Nina killed Dwight."

"Fat lot of good that did anyone," Maggie snapped. "Notice how she only killed him when it was *her* problem, when *she* was the one who was in trouble. When it was Sienna, she couldn't care less. She deserved what she got."

"Did you know she was going to kill him?" Kidd asked

"What?"

"Did you know that Nina was planning on killing Dwight?"

Maggie swallowed. "No," she said. "I... I didn't know."

And Kidd saw it, saw right through it all. "So you were hoping that because you knew she was being threatened by him, that her death would be pinned on him. And then everything would be okay? You'd get away with it."

"I was so careful," Maggie said. "I covered my face, my hands, I didn't leave a single trace anywhere. It would have been easy. And then... Then he was found dead."

"And Harper?"

"She went to tell you things," Maggie said. "I saw her coming out of the police station entirely by chance and I knew, I just knew that she would have said something that would leave my sister in the shit. I couldn't take that chance. I couldn't. So she had to go too."

"She didn't say a thing," Kidd said. He was almost enjoying this. "She told us about Dwight, she helped lead us to him if nothing else. You killed her for nothing."

"I... I couldn't take that chance."

Kidd looked at her, looked at Sienna, looked to the door where DS Sanchez was standing, other members of the team just behind her. He didn't know how much of this conversation they'd heard, but he'd heard enough to know what had happened, to know what he'd missed, to know that she was going to go down for this. Sienna, too. Maggie had done all this to avenge her sister, to avenge her family, and now she'd got herself in more trouble than she could ever hope to get herself out of.

"Send the officers in," Kidd said to Sanchez. "This is over."

CHAPTER
FORTY

Kidd made his way towards his house, feeling like the eyes of the world were on him as he walked through town, as people made their way out of work to the local pubs to soak up some alcohol as the week slowly inched towards its end. It was getting on for five pm as he left the station, and his progress through town was slow. He didn't want to think about what he looked like, didn't want to think about what a wreck he must have seemed to anyone that he was passing on the street. It was embarrassing.

The weather had started to turn once again. Where the day had managed to stay somewhat bright, if a bit cloudy, the sky was now a threatening, deathly grey, and was pelting his head with little raindrops.

The case was over. It would be wrapped up in the

coming days with interviews, with statements. He had sent officers to the flat to get Bailey's body out of there, to take her to get an autopsy done. They had contacted next of kin, told her family they would need to identify the body. It was all so bloody horrible, and all so preventable.

He messaged John to let him know what had happened, that he was finished, and that he was on his way home. The response was almost instant.

JOHN: Take your time. Don't rush. Be careful. I'm making food.

He was lucky to have him. So bloody lucky to have him.

He walked through town, past the riverside where Nina had been found earlier that week. The flowers were wilting, the note cards were curling at the edges, the moisture in the air making the ink run. Soon it would be cleared away, soon it would be forgotten, at least for the people in the immediate vicinity. There were people who would carry that loss forever, though.

He walked past The Snake Pit. It would be open again by the weekend. It would go back to how things were before, the parties, the life it had before Nina's was taken away. He walked past the spot where he'd had the shit kicked out of him the night before. Everything still hurt, ached beyond ache. He didn't even feel like he should have been upright. It was adrenaline that had carried him through the afternoon, of that much he was entirely certain.

He stopped suddenly.

Waiting on the corner, a stone's throw from Kidd's house, he saw Craig Peyton. The difference this time was that he was actually waiting for him, and there was a duffel bag at his side. He was leaving once again it seemed. How long had he been waiting there? Had he gone to the house first? Christ, he hoped he hadn't gone to the house first.

"Going somewhere nice?" Kidd asked.

"Do you really want to know?"

Kidd shook his head. "You know what? I don't," Kidd replied. "Wherever it is, keep yourself safe."

"I will," he said. "You look like shit."

"Thanks," Kidd said.

"What happened?"

"You really want to know?"

"Yes," Craig said. "Doesn't mean you have to tell me, though."

"Okay," Kidd replied. "Sorry if you thought I was accusing you of killing Nina."

"It's okay."

"You show up unannounced—"

"I was hardly going to announce it to you."

"So you could have the drama of floating into my life like some kind of ghost?" Kidd asked.

"Something like that," Craig replied with a smirk.

"I'm just saying," Kidd said. "You show up unannounced and are involved in the case in some way, and then I've got Andrea at my back wanting to know where you are."

"You could have told her."

"I didn't know where you were," Kidd said. "I didn't lie to her. But that's a reason not to tell me where you're going. You didn't tell me last time, don't tell me this time. I don't want you getting in any kind of trouble because of me. And vice versa."

Craig blinked. "What do you mean?"

"I don't want any part of whatever unfinished business you've got going on," Kidd said. "That's the last thing I want. So... next time, if there's going to be a next time, just keep me out of it."

Craig seemed a little surprised by this, and Kidd couldn't help but wonder what he thought he was going to get out of this conversation. Did he want forgiveness? Did he want Kidd to go with him? That had been the suggestion last time, hadn't it? When he'd left all those months ago, he'd wanted Kidd to drop everything and go on the run with him. But things had changed. Everything had shifted. Kidd had a life here, a life he was pretty happy with, all things considered. He didn't need Craig anymore. He was ready to draw a line under it. At least, that's what he told himself.

"Okay," Craig said. "I guess this is goodbye, then."

"Did you tie up your loose ends?" Kidd asked.

Craig smiled. "Yes, I did," he replied. "I'm all set. I won't need to come back."

He stepped forward and went to hug Kidd. Kidd pulled him in, holding him close, knowing, or at least hoping, that this would be the last time they said goodbye to one another. This truly was the end. It had to be.

"Safe travels," Kidd said.

"Good luck," Craig replied.

Craig picked up his duffel bag and started towards town. Kidd didn't know where he was going, probably to the train station, maybe to get an Uber or a taxi from somewhere. But he didn't want to know. He wanted him out of his life, and if you'd told him that a year ago, he would have called you crazy.

Kidd started back towards his house. He took out his key and opened the front door. The light was on in the kitchen, John standing at the stove cooking something that smelled so delicious that Kidd could feel the very scent of it penetrating his bones, making him feel better. It looked like stew.

"What's that?" Kidd asked.

"That's lunch. Or dinner. I don't know. You've not eaten," John said. "Breakfast?"

"Weird breakfast."

"Did you see him?" John asked.

"What?"

"Craig," John said. "He came over."

"When?"

"Half an hour ago," John said. "I told him to wait inside, but he didn't want to. Said he didn't feel comfortable doing that... Like I felt comfortable with him doing that, I was just trying to be nice."

"Sorry. He just left."

"You're not," John said. "But I get it. Did you... Did you manage to help?"

"All tied up."

"Good."

They were standing at opposite ends of the kitchen, neither one of them apparently willing to close the space.

"So is that the end?" John asked.

He looked so hurt, and Kidd couldn't help but wonder how much he'd seen. If he'd been looking out the window, he would have seen them hug. That would explain why he looked like he was about to shatter into a thousand pieces.

"Yes," Kidd said. "He's going. He won't be coming back."

"I thought he said that last time," John replied. "And here we are again, doing the same dance."

"I don't want to fight with you about this."

"And I don't want to keep doubting our relationship every time he comes up," John said. "If it's not him, it's one of his friends, or even his sister. I don't know where I stand sometimes in your rankings."

"You're top of the list."

"Then you need to start making me feel like it,"

John said. "Because I do feel like that a lot of the time, but then he shows up and it's like I don't even matter. You derail everything for him. He shows up and... and just his presence threatens to spoil what we have."

"I know," Kidd said. "I don't want that either. Believe me, I don't."

"Okay," John said. "I want all of you, Ben. I don't want to share you with a past that just won't stay away."

"I know that," Kidd said. "I want you, too. All of you. I don't want him; I've not wanted him for a long time. When we were first going out, I wanted to know he was safe, I wanted to know that he was doing okay, and yes, that made things complicated for us. And then when we were away, it reared its ugly head again, and I am trying so hard not to let it get in the way of us. I really am." Kidd sighed. "My life is just complicated."

"I know," John said. "I don't think I knew what I was letting myself in for."

Kidd didn't know what to say to that. The implication was, of course, that maybe he would have chosen not to be with Kidd if he'd known about all of the drama that would ensue. But he didn't want to tug at that thread. He was worried that if he gave John an out, he would take it, and Kidd would be left all alone again. He didn't want that. He didn't want that, especially if it meant losing John.

"I can't promise you no drama," Kidd said, stepping towards him, tentatively, not wanting to spook him, like he was approaching a wild animal. "But how about low drama? Or lower drama?"

"I don't think you can promise me low drama, Ben," John said. "Have you met yourself? You attract it."

"I know," Kidd said. "But I don't want you getting caught in the crossfire of it."

"Me neither."

Kidd pulled him into a hug, and they stood there in the kitchen of his house for some time.

Cars whizzed by on the main road, the rain continued to drizzle outside, and Kidd and John just held one another, like they were the only thing keeping each other upright.

Kidd didn't know where things were going. He had no idea what was going to happen next. Life felt unsteady, and he didn't like it. He didn't like it one bit. But he had John, and that made all the difference.

At least they had each other.

ABOUT THE AUTHOR

GS Rhodes has been writing for as long as he can remember, scribbling stories on spare bits of paper and hoping to one day share those stories with the world. The DI Benjamin Kidd series is GS Rhodes first foray into crime writing, combining a love of where he has lived for a lot of his life with his love of a good mystery. Now well into this series, he is also writing a spin-off featuring DS Zoe Sanchez in the starring role, starting with Deadly Tears.

facebook.com/Gsrhodesauthor

instagram.com/gs_rhodes

DI BENJAMIN KIDD WILL
RETURN IN

UNLUCKY FOR SOME

(Coming 2025)

Printed in Dunstable, United Kingdom

65661481R00180